One f

Tales fron.   ᴐon

Edited by

Roo B. Doo

and

H.K. Hillman

The Eleventh Underdog Anthology from Leg Iron Books

Spring 2020

Disclaimer

These stories are works of fiction. Characters, names, places and incidents are either the product of the authors' imaginations or are used in a fictitious context. Any resemblance to any persons, living or dead, or to any events or locales is entirely coincidental. If any of the events described have really happened to you then I'm afraid that's your own problem.

Copyright notice

LEG IRON BOOKS

https://legironbooks.co.uk/

Cover image © H. K. Hillman

ISBN: 9798644854233

Contents

Foreword

H. K. Hillman

Eleven is the number of magick, according to Aleister Crowley. That particular spelling of magick was his invention too, despite the protestations of current followers of New Age practices. Sorry folks, it doesn't all originate from the Light Side.

Well here we are at Anthology Eleven and I must admit it feels pretty magical to me. I remember when it felt optimistic to name the first anthology 'Volume One' and promise three a year, every year. And yet, here we are.

So far, every anthology has included at least one new author and this time we have Wandra Nomad to introduce. Wandra has her own collection of short stories in the works at Leg Iron Books, titled 'Musings of a Wanderer'.

This anthology is later than it should have been because 2020 has been a year of one disaster after another. As well as most of the world being in lockdown because of a virus. Hence the title of this volume.

It would have been later still if Roo B. Doo had not taken on the bulk of the editing. Nonetheless, it does contain fourteen stories from nine authors, a mix of everything from the whimsical to the horrifying, something for everyone. I hope you find something to enjoy in these pages.

Finally, I would like to dedicate this anthology to my father, Albert John Hillman, who died suddenly in February this year. At least he has been spared the insanity that has gripped the world since then.

The Meteorite

Mark Ellott

Chicxulub, late Cretaceous, sixty-five million years ago.⊐⊐⊐⊐⊐⊐⊐⊐⊐⊐⊐⊐⊐⊐⊐⊐⊐⊐⊐

Triceratops lifted his great horned head and paused from his munching. Chewing the foliage in his mouth, he sniffed the air, his snorts loud in the silence of the morning. Somewhere beneath the dense bone that constituted his skull with its three menacing horns that raked the air as he moved his head from side to side, a thought stirred.

It wasn't much of a thought, for he had little brain matter with which to think. Mostly it concentrated on where was the best place to find good eating and keeping away from predators, otherwise it was just vague senses. However, something triggered in the synapses and he pondered as best he could on what it was with what brain power that he had, which was much like a surgeon attempting to conduct brain surgery when all he has to hand is a club hammer. A feeling that something was different. That was it—something different.

The sky was a clear, cloudless blue yet there was something else. A tiny dot far above the planet that could have been another, smaller sun. It shouldn't be there. It wasn't there before and now it was and even in the dim recesses of Triceratops' dense skull, it foreboded something ominous.

Triceratops twisted his head to look at the dot as it grew larger. Something akin to curiosity passed through his mind. As the seconds passed, the dot grew bright in the sky, trailing a plume of burning matter as it entered the atmosphere and Triceratops watched it.

A few seconds later, the meteorite struck the shallow sea and plunged deep into the Earth's crust, thrusting clouds of molten rock and dust high into the atmosphere. The shockwave crashed out from the epicentre of the strike carrying a firestorm in its wake.

Triceratops barely had time to process the events in his tiny brain. He was incinerated where he stood. He was fortunate, for his end was quick. One minute he was alive and the next he was vaporised. Some sixty-five million years later, palaeontologists would pick over the fossilised remains of his bones, evidence of this devastating moment, frozen in the time strata of the rocks.

The plume of gypsum and dust spiralled up into the atmosphere as the shock wave dissipated over the continent.

A thousand miles north, the herd of Hadrosaur ambled across the landscape, wary of any roaming Tyrannosaurs. Lifting their heads and sniffing the air, constantly checking for the apex predator who may, at any moment, strike one of their number. The herd was confident that there was safety in numbers and they were right, for it was not Tyrannosaurus who would seal their fate.

One of the lookouts lifted his head and looked at the southern sky and the strange light on the horizon. Like Triceratops, he sensed something wrong, but his capacity for thought was limited; far too limited to process what was happening miles away to the south. The shock wave was little more than a tremor, and Hadrosaur was familiar with those. He thought nothing of it and returned to foraging for food, having sensed no sign of Tyrannosaurus.

The sky grew dark.

With the dark, came the cold.

Days passed. Weeks came and went. Months merged into each other and still the darkness enveloped the Earth with its icy embrace.

The leaves died and food became scarce.

As the days and weeks drifted by, the Hadrosaurs sought food but to no avail. One by one they fell to the famine and their carcasses were temporary respite for the scavengers and carnivores.

In the seas, the Mosasaurs struggled to find food. One by one, they faded away, starved to death. On the land, the Tyrannosaurs picked clean the bones of the herbivores and looked for more, but there were no more to be found and they too fell victim to the cold famine.

One lone Velociraptor looked up at the ominous sky and his belly ached for food that wasn't to be found. Deep inside he knew he was doomed and he felt something akin to lament for the passing of a dynasty and a future that would never be his.

And the sky remained dark. The Earth went into hibernation and the reptiles died. Velociraptor laid his weary head down and closed his eyes, never to open them again. The desolate, dead landscape was cast into eternal shadow. Nothing moved.

When the dust eventually fell from the sky the sun shone through again. The plants came to life, covering the bleak landscape with lush green foliage, but it was too late for the dinosaurs, for they had gone.

Alphadon moved out into the new world. Now that the dinosaurs were no more, he would—along with the other mammals—inherit the Earth. One day, his descendants would be the apex predators and command the world and all that is in it. He sniffed the air and set about hunting for food. Life was good.

Sometime in the future

Jonathan Shepard hated this bit. He sat back in the seat and buckled himself in. It didn't matter how many times he made the trip, this part—leaving the atmosphere—was always the same. The G forces made him feel sick and he hated it. He glanced across at his companion. She hadn't said much despite his attempts to engage her in light conversation. Colonel Mathilda Burgess was USAF and her military background set her apart from Jonathan who had spent his early career evading both the military and the law when running blockades. These days he was a respectable pilot, but she knew about his past and made no attempt to disguise her distaste.

I'm just the taxi driver, he mused irritably to himself. This mission was her mission and he had been left with no illusions that he was second fiddle. *Just get her there and back,* he had been told.

My kite, my navigation and my expertise getting us there, count for nothing. She's the bleedin' weapons expert and without her, there is no mission.

It occurred to him to mention at one point that each role was as important as the other.

She had looked at him through her cold dark eyes, stiffened slightly, and increasing her stature by an inch or so as she responded. "You do your job, Mr Shepard and I'll do mine. We shall get along just fine."

Just fine to colonel Burgess, it seemed to him, was more like two ice cubes rubbing along in a freezer compartment. Their mission was to be dangerous enough without a potentially hostile relationship.

Still, he thought, they would be back soon enough.

The countdown started and the knot in his stomach tightened.

He looked again at Burgess, but she was staring ahead and didn't meet his eye. She showed no outward symptoms of stress even though this was to be her first space flight.

"Hold tight," he said in an attempt to lighten the atmosphere between them.

"There is no need for false levity, Mr Shepard. I am perfectly calm."

"Suit yourself. It's Jonathan, by the way."

"Thank you, I will... Jonathan."

The countdown finished and the craft lifted into the air, the whole vehicle shaking under the pressure from the thrust. The two occupants fell silent and concentrated on their own internal worlds as the G forces pushed them back into their seats.

Eventually, they were free of the atmosphere and the ageing shuttle was under Shepard's control. Thankful to be out of the G forces, he started to breathe again. "Everything okay?" he asked as he turned the controls towards the International Space Station.

"Yes, thank you."

She lapsed into silence again and Shephard concentrated on navigating the short distance to the docking port on the side of the structure. The shuttle engaged with a satisfying clunk and the door between the two hissed open.

Shepard unbuckled his seat belt and Burgess did likewise. They made their way to the port.

"They've got the new artificial gravity installed, I see," he said.

"Mmm."

Shephard shrugged and walked along the corridor to the briefing room. Colonel Burgess may not be impressed, he thought, but it made a pleasant change from weightlessness for him and he appreciated the sensation nonetheless. He led the way to the conference room and pressed the button. The door slid open with a hiss. There was a small group of people waiting, seated around a long table at the end of which was a viewscreen. One of them stood and reached out a hand. "Hello, Jonathan. This must be Colonel Burgess?"

Jonathan took the proffered hand. "Frank."

"Mathilda Burgess," she took Frank's hand after Jonathan.

"Frank Connor, Director of Operations," he said. "I'm running this mission." He gestured to two chairs. "Please, sit."

Pleasantries over, they sat and watched as Frank Connor switched on a display on one wall. "The reason you two are here is to prevent this meteorite from reaching Earth," he started. "Its current trajectory will have it strike somewhere around the Gulf of Mexico in about five days' time..."

"Four days, twenty three hours, fifteen minutes and fifty-nine seconds," a thin man with rimless spectacles interrupted.

Frank smiled. "Geoffrey Walker, our analyst," he said.

They nodded at the man and Frank continued. "It is currently travelling at forty thousand miles per hour. You have to go out and destroy it before it gets here." He turned to Burgess. "That is your job."

She nodded.

"And you understand fully what is required?"

"I have been briefed," she said.

"Something I want you to see," Frank continued, zooming the image so that they should see the meteor.

"What is that?" Jonathan asked.

"Ah, yes, we wondered if you would ask that. The answer is, we do not know."

As they looked at the enlarged image, they could see what appeared to be a ring, with darker space on the inside surrounded by what looked like tiny dots of light.

"We think it might just be a ring of space dust reflecting light from the sun," Walker said. "But despite sending out probes, we cannot be certain."

"How big is it?" Jonathan asked, thinking that perhaps going around it might be an option.

"Over half a light year, so if you are thinking what I suspect you are thinking, then no, you will have to go through it. Whatever 'it' is."

Jonathan squinted as he looked at the image; a ring with the meteorite a glowing dot in the middle. "The space inside the ring appears to be slightly darker and the stars... There's something odd about them, but I can't quite decide what it is."

"Nevertheless," Burgess said. "We will fly through it tomorrow, so we will find out then." She glanced at her watch. "Is there anything else that you wish to brief us on gentlemen?"

Frank shook his head. "You are the weapons expert, Colonel, so we leave that part of the mission to you."

"Very good." She stood. "Then, captain Shephard, I suggest that we get some rest. We will leave at 06:00 tomorrow."

Jonathan rose at 05:30. Showered, shaved and ate a small breakfast. As he walked to the dock, Burgess was there already and waiting. They entered the shuttle and fastened their seatbelts.

Jonathan went through the pre-flight check and spoke briefly to flight control. The shuttle disconnected from the space station and turned in the direction of the oncoming meteorite.

Well, this is it.

They sat in silence as he piloted the craft to its rendezvous with the nine mile wide lump of rock hurtling towards the Earth. It would take precise navigation to get themselves in a position where Burgess could launch the missiles from the adapted shuttle. Given the limited time available since the discovery of the meteorite, the adaptations were somewhat hurried and there had been no time to carry out full testing, so they were in unknown territory. The meteor was moving at 40,000 miles per hour in what could best be described as an eccentric flight pattern as it rotated.

"The meteorite has a weak point about midway along its length," she had said during the briefing. "If the missile strikes at that point, it should shatter."

"Should?"

She shrugged. "It is not a precise science. We do not know the full makeup of the rock, nor how strong it is. But that's our best bet."

They flew in silence with each absorbed with their own thoughts until they came to the anomaly that they had observed from the probes the day before.

"Well," Jonathan said. "I was right, the space is different. This is not a ring of space dust, it's more like…"

"A tear in fabric."

"Yes, precisely." He paused in thought as they looked at the anomaly. "So space is not a linear thing. This is a rip in its fabric—as you say. Fascinating."

They looked at the anomaly as it loomed ahead of them, millions of tiny dots of light around the edge as if space itself had been ripped apart.

"Fascinating it may be," she said, "but we have a job to do."

"Aye, aye," he responded, increasing the thrust.

Before long, they were through.

"There's something about the stars," Jonathan reflected. "Not quite sure what it is…"

"They do seem brighter."

"Mmm, something else. They aren't quite where I would expect them to be."

They lapsed into silence as Jonathan brought the shuttle into range of the meteorite. A small pin prick of light in the blackness that lazily twisted on its axis as it moved towards the Earth. Despite travelling at 40,000 miles per hour, it appeared to be moving gently through the void. With nothing against which to gauge its travel, to the naked eye, it barely appeared to move at all.

"Bring me to within 20,000 klicks," Mathilda instructed.

"Aye, aye."

Jonathan swung the shuttle round so that they were closing in on the meteor from the starboard side.

"A little closer…"

He obeyed and opened the thrusters, making slight adjustments to the trajectory.

"A little more. Another thousand klicks."

"Aye, aye."

"Okay, that should do." She reached down and pressed the launch button. A torpedo shot forward towards its target. They watched as it struck the meteorite in the middle section. There was a small explosion as the projectile bounced off the meteorite and exploded harmlessly into space.

"Dammit!"

Jonathan looked across at her, but refrained from comment. This was always going to be a tricky assignment and they had more torpedoes on board in readiness for a failure.

"Move us a little closer and to starboard. Five degrees."

He followed her instructions.

"Okay, try again."

Another torpedo sped towards the spinning lump of rock. It struck in the middle. There was a pause then a blinding light as the torpedo exploded. For a second, they could see nothing on the view screen. Then as the light dissipated, there was nothing.

"Wait for it," he said.

A minute or so later, the millions of particles bounced off the shuttle's hull, battering it like rain. Then silence. He did a quick systems check, but he could see no sign of damage.

"Mission accomplished, I think," he said.

She smiled. It was the first time he had ever seen Mathilda Burgess smile. She nodded then. "Time to go home."

Jonathan turned the shuttle and headed back to the anomaly.

"That's odd," he said.

"I see it. It's shrinking."

"Rapidly, too." He increased thrust and the shuttle surged forward as the opening continued to shrink. As they passed through it, he turned the craft to look as the anomaly finally sealed itself.

"A few moments later and we would have been stuck on the far side of that."

"Wherever that was."

"Indeed. I guess we will never know now."

He resumed course for the space station and manoeuvred the shuttle alongside.

"That's strange."

"What?"

"Look," he said. "The markings have changed."

She frowned and followed his gaze.

"Curious. The national flags are gone. I don't recognise those markings at all."

Jonathan felt the hairs on the back of his neck tingle.

"I don't like the smell of it."

He lined the shuttle up and nosed it into the dock. Everything seemed to be working fine, but those hairs still stood up. They disembarked and walked into the station.

"My God, it's hot in here."

Burgess nodded. "Must be over thirty degrees. Stifling."

They looked about but the corridor was deserted. Slowly they made their way to the briefing room. Once there, Jonathan pressed the button and the door hissed open.

They stood then, staring at what faced them. Alien beings. About their own height but reptilian with long snouts and rows of pointed teeth and a downy feathery covering on their scaly skin. Their bodies were slender and lithe with slim arms and legs. There was something both menacing and agile about how these creatures held themselves as if ready to leap into action against a foe at any instant, yet, they also appeared relaxed beneath the outward appearance.

One of the aliens sitting around the table got up and reached out a clawed hand. He spoke in gibberish.

Jonathan tried to respond. "Who are you? What are you doing here? Where is Frank Connor?"

The alien said something unintelligible, but it seemed to Jonathan that he was gesturing for him to speak again.

"I said, what is going on here…"

"Ah," said the alien, "the translator has picked up enough to start analysing your language. You can understand me?"

Jonathan nodded. "What is going on?"

"You must be the warm bloods. We have been waiting for you. It was foretold that you would arrive through a hole from another world. Our ancient scrolls tell of warm bloods who saved our kind from extinction by destroying the great light in the sky that was set to crash into the planet and wipe out all life. But many did not believe that warm bloods could evolve into beings that can travel the stars. But we believed. We waited and our wait has been rewarded. What planet are you from?"

"This one. Earth."

"Earth? What is Earth? Where is that?"

"Here!" Jonathan gestured to the blue planet below them, visible in the window. *"Here!"*

"Terra? No that is where *we* come from."

Burgess drew a short inward breath and grasped Jonathan by the sleeve, pulling him to one side.

"Shit!" She said. "That anomaly…"

"Yes, what of it?"

"I don't think it was a tear in the fabric of space. Look at them. Look closely. What do they remind you of?"

Jonathan turned to the aliens. Slowly as he looked, he realised that there was something vaguely familiar about these beings. Something that he had seen in books and horror films. Something that was both fascinating and scary at the same time. The intelligent reptiles that hunted remorselessly in fiction and fact. Apex predators that once roamed the Earth millions of years ago.

"Velociraptor!"

"Yes. You know of our ancestors," the alien explained. "A long time ago now. We have evolved from such simple beings. Look around you. We have mastered space travel. Soon we will travel the stars as your kind do."

"It wasn't a tear in space," Burgess repeated, "It was a tear in time. There was no second meteorite. There was only ever the one. And we destroyed it. We have changed time. The dinosaurs are still the masters of the Earth."

"That's why the stars were different." He turned to velociraptor. "But what of us?"

The velociraptor smiled, showing his rows of sharp teeth. "There are some creatures much like you in our southern continents. A simple species, they tend to remain in the trees, though. They will never develop into an intelligent species I fear. They lack the brain capacity. The other warm bloods we farm for food."

The Trade

Mark Ellott

Pascale Hervé stepped off the motorcycle and walked up to the police crime scene tape. A uniformed officer barred her way.

"Sergeant Patrice Laurent is expecting me," she explained.

The man lifted his radio and asked for Patrice. Pascale's curious gaze scanned her surroundings—old habits die hard, she thought to herself. This was one of the smart suburbs of Lodève and an unusual location for a fatality involving the police. The gentle afternoon sun illuminated well-to-do properties and the general sense of peace and tranquillity was at odds with the gaggle of police cars, crime scene investigators and the incongruous tape cordoning off the area from passers-by.

A few moments later Patrice arrived at the tape and told the man to let her through. "Pascale, how are you?" he asked, briefly embracing her.

"I am managing," she said.

"I was sorry to hear about Guillaume. I would have come to the funeral, but I was called away. Work... You understand."

She understood all too well, as that had been her working life until two years previously. Then semi-retirement and supposedly more time with Guillaume. Until prostate cancer took him before his time. The retirement never happened and she felt cheated. Angry, resentful, and, yes, cheated and now, so alone.

"What is it that you called me here for?" She asked, pushing the personal thoughts from her mind.

"Ah, yes, come here, I have something to show you."

He led the way into the building and up the stairs to the first floor apartment. Inside was a scene of devastation. Smashed furniture lay discarded across the room along with the contents of cupboards and drawers. In the middle of the chaos, was the victim. He walked over to where the body lay and beckoned Pascale to join him. There was blood spread across the tiled floor and the broken body was contorted at an unnatural angle.

A woman in her fifties, Pascale guessed. *Surprised a burglar, perhaps*, she thought. *Going by the blood and the wound in her abdomen, stabbed*. She gasped as she looked closer.

She reached for the woman's arm and felt for a pulse. Nothing. But the eyes. She lifted a finger and moved it back and forth above the dead woman's face and the eyes followed it. Reaching into her pocket she pulled out a small flashlight and shone it directly at the woman's eyes and watched the pupils contract.

"*Merde*! Not again," she breathed.

"So, you have seen this before," Patrice said.

Pascale looked up at him. She had, but he shouldn't be able to recall. It was all supposed to have been put right. No one should have remembered.

"I have this feeling…" he started. "This feeling that I've seen it before, but I cannot quite remember."

Pascale stood. This wasn't right. She clenched her fists and relaxed them, her normally tanned face now exhibiting a pallor.

"What do you remember?" she asked.

"I am not sure. Just that I have seen this undead thing before."

He paused. "You know what it is, don't you?"

"Unfortunately, I do. What bothers me is that you have a memory of this. You should not have remembered anything."

"So what is it?"

She sighed. He wouldn't believe her if she did tell him. "I have to go," she said. "I need to see someone about this. Leave it with me."

"Pascale!"

Patrice watched as she retreated. He heard her footsteps on the stairs.

"*Merde!*"

He went over to the window and watched her as she walked across the grass and made her way back to the bike. She mounted it, pressed the starter button and was gone, the muffled exhaust sound all that she left. Patrice frowned. She knew something and it bothered him. It bothered him that she knew what it was that he was now dealing with. Why wouldn't she tell him?

"Pah!" He said to himself. Then, "get the body to the morgue," to the SOC investigator who happened to be in the room and caught the brunt of his irritation.

"Yes, sir."

Pascale pulled the bike up at the side of the road and looked across to her right. She remembered this place. So long ago now, but it hadn't changed. Sand blown in from the sea drifted across the road and she felt her foot slipping on it as she steadied the bike, placing the sidestand down and resting the machine's weight on it before stepping off. She removed her helmet and placed it in one of the panniers before the sand had time to get into the mechanism. Already she could feel the grittiness on her face as the particles skipped along with the breeze.

The Mediterranean air carried with it the tang of salt and seaweed and she breathed deeply, savouring its essence. Above, the gulls keened and squabbled. On the sandy beach were two deckchairs. They faced out to sea where the turquoise waves gently lapped the shore. She didn't fully understand how she got here, as when she left Patrice, she had just ridden, expecting much the same thing to happen as had happened previously and sure enough, here she was. She looked down to the beach and saw the scythe leaning against one of the deckchairs, its occupant's back to her, but she recognised the familiar outline.

She walked down to the deckchairs, her mind aware of the difficulty of walking on loose sand in motorcycle boots. As she drew level, Death turned and looked at her. Two glowing eyes bored into her soul.

"Ah, Pascale. Nice to see you again. Do sit down," he gestured to the empty chair and she slumped into it.

Death reached down and lifted up a bottle of wine and proffered it to her. *"Pégairolles,"* he said. *"You are partial, I recall."*

"Thank you." She took the bottle and poured some into a glass that Death had left by the deckchair. She took a sip and savoured the warm fruity flavour. "What are you up to?" She asked.

"Up to?" Death feigned confusion.

"You know what I mean. The undead bodies. We've been here before. That Christmas a few years back. When you thought it would be okay to go swanning off drinking and smoking and leave the work behind. That '*up to*'," she said flatly.

"Ah, yes, that." He took a sip of wine himself before fishing into his cape and pulling out a packet of cigarettes. He put one into his mouth and flicked a zippo, igniting the end. He drew deeply and breathed out a plume of smoke. *"Yes, that."*

For a moment they sat in companionable silence, neither seeking to break the gentle mood of the bay and the sea breaking on the sandy shore. The gulls were still shrieking above, but otherwise it was peaceful. Death had all the time in the world, Pascale presumed and she was in no hurry to get him to speak, for she had time on her hands as well.

Eventually he broke the silence. *"Tell me what happened."*

"Patrice called me to a crime scene."

"So much for retirement then."

"Indeed."

"Why?"

"I think you know why. The undead." She turned to look directly at him, eyeball to glowing eye socket. If she hoped to shame him into admitting any fault, she was to be disappointed. He took a drag on his cigarette, before snuffing out the dog end and dropping it on the sand and rubbing his foot on it, pushing it down into the sand and out of sight. Pascale frowned, but before she could chide him, he interjected. *"I'm a supernatural being. It's a supernatural cigarette, so no harm, eh?"*

She laughed briefly. "So what is going on?"

I'm taking a holiday. One gets tired working all the hours, don't you know?"

"I do, but you are a supernatural being. I would have thought such things didn't apply to you. Besides. Patrice remembered last time."

Death started and looked at her.

Ah, she thought. *You didn't expect that, did you?*

Death took another sip of the wine before holding it up to the light. *"A pleasant enough drink, but I prefer a single malt."* He returned to the subject. *"Tell me."*

"The reason he called me was because he remembered something. He couldn't recall all the detail, just that he remembered something

22

like this before—undead bodies. And he knew that I had been involved. But you were supposed to tidy up. It would seem that you didn't."

Death sighed. *"I didn't expect that. Still, he won't remember anything when I have gone back to correct things."*

"You had better. I could do without being called back."

Death waved a hand in dismissal. *"I will sort it out, don't you worry."*

Pascale sipped the wine and looked across at him again. Something wasn't quite right. "You summoned me here, didn't you?"

Death smiled. She wondered how he did that, given that he had no flesh.

"You were always perceptive, Pascale. It's what I like about you."

"So all this was a ruse to get me here." It was a statement rather than a question.

"The space time continuum is a sensitive thing. Little ripples spread out and I can feel them. Much like the spider in the centre of her web when the fly strikes it. I feel those tiny disturbances each and every one. And I detected yours."

For a moment, she said nothing. Then eventually, "go on."

"How is that retirement going?" He countered.

She sighed heavily and took another sip, savoured the liquid and swallowed.

"Not so good, then?"

"You figured."

"One of the benefits of being omniscient."

She sighed again. "Retirement, everyone said, was a new beginning. A transition from the old to the new. A chance to take things a little more slowly, to savour time and to do things that I enjoy."

She drifted into silence as she took another sip of the Pégairolles. Even the taste of the wine brought a lump to her throat. This place carried memories of a time long gone, a happier time.

"But Guillaume died."

"Yes. Guillaume died. And you would have known that when you encouraged me to choose life, to grasp it by the throat, to squeeze every drop of essence from it, to live, to love and to thrive. Two years later, I am alone, empty and heartbroken. Have you any idea what it is like to wake in an empty bed knowing that this is to be another day without that person you spent your life with? To go to bed at night knowing that you leave yet another day between you and them as they fade into the past, out of reach forever, an echo in your mind? Do you? *Do you?!*"

"No. I cannot. But I do not always see what is to happen. It doesn't work that way. I get notified and I go to collect the dead. I do not have their lives at my fingertips. The space time continuum is about a feeling, not certainty. I was not to know that it would be so soon and for that, I am sorry, really I am."

"I thought you were omniscient."

Death shrugged. *"Well, I see things. Feel them more like, but I am not aware of every tiny detail—it's more of an overview, if you like. Perhaps, mostly omniscient…"*

She snapped her head round to treat him to one of her stares. "How on earth can you be mostly omniscient? Either you are or you are not."

Death remained unruffled. *"I am a supernatural being…"*

"Your go-to response when caught out," she said flatly.

They lapsed into silence again as Death realised that she was right, but didn't pursue the matter. She would tell him what was on her mind eventually and he was content to let the conversation evolve organically. Of all the mortals that he had dealings with, it was Pascale who had caused him the most difficulty and it troubled him, despite his liking for her.

"I can't go on like this," she was saying, bringing him back from his reverie.

"I understand. But while you are alive, there is hope. There is a future. You may find another."

"I do not want another. It will never be the same."

"No, not the same, but you can enjoy a different life."

"All I see is darkness. An emptiness that stretches out before me. I could live for decades yet and I cannot cope."

Death fished in his cape and pulled out his smartphone. He tapped at the screen. *"Hmmm."*

"What does "hmmm" mean?"

24

"Well, decades is not so very far off."

Pascale watched the waves drifting into the shore, myriad points of light dancing on the surface. Even this place wasn't right. It was exactly as she remembered it. And that was the point. Since then it had changed as commerce moved in and took advantage of the tourism opportunities. Now it had ice cream parlours and burger vans, shops selling plastic tat for the visitors, and the beach should have been full of the latter. *Not to mention litter,* she thought irritably. Here, though, in this moment, it was exactly as it had been on the long ride south that day thirty years ago. Just an empty cove with the Mediterranean lapping at the soft silvery sand. Even the sun remained where it was, somewhere in the late afternoon. By now it should have moved westwards and lower over the horizon, yet it remained frozen in time and space. A space that existed only in her memory.

"Time heals," Death was saying.

"Trite, clichéd nonsense," she snapped. "Time merely opens up the wound. Time pulls me further away while he is stuck in the ever disappearing past, lost beyond reach, while I move further away into the future, desolate, broken, lonely and longing for peace. Time has done no healing for me. Time has merely made my loss more acute. Every night I go to bed hoping that I will not wake to face another futile day."

"So what do you expect of me?"

"Take me as you were supposed to all that time ago. Put right the anomaly that you manipulated. I am ready now. There is nothing left here for me."

Death sighed one of his sonorous, universe shaking sighs. *"I cannot."*

"Why? You managed to change things once before. You should have taken me long ago, before all this pain. But you changed time. If you did it then, why can you not do it now?"

"It is precisely because I did it then, that I cannot do it now. Those ripples…" He lapsed into silence.

"What about them?"

"I am not the only one who can feel them, my dear. I have made subtle changes and no one has noticed, but if I keep doing it, sooner

or later they will and I will be in a great deal of trouble. I simply cannot take the risk again."

They lapsed into an awkward silence, sipping wine and still the sun remained high in the sky and still the light danced on the waves and still the seagulls wheeled overhead. He lit another cigarette and she watched as the smoke trickled upwards and dispersed into the air. Everything was surreal to her. The light was a little too bright, the sounds a little too clear, the sea a little too blue, the sand a little too silvery. It was a dream-like sense of reality, a facsimile of the real thing, a distortion of memory.

"This isn't real."

"No."

She pondered the thought for a moment. "None of it is."

"No."

Then it occurred to her that she had everything back to front. "You didn't summon me, did you?"

"No."

Death remained silent as she worked through her thoughts aloud. "I summoned you."

"Yes."

"Patrice, the undead bodies, the ride here. It's all in my head…"

"Well done."

"But why?"

"You have a question to consider. A decision to make and speaking to you here, in this place—well, your head—is somewhere that we can do it."

"I don't want to go on. I cannot face the interminable years alone."

"You don't have to. You may meet someone else."

"But it wouldn't be the same."

"No."

"And you won't take me, so I have to go on."

Death stubbed out the cigarette. *"There is another option. I had hoped to avoid it. I had hoped that you would come through this. However, it seems that you will not be persuaded. So…"*

"What is it?"

He told her.

"Of course, there is no going back if you choose this path. So take your time to consider. There is no rush…"

"I don't need time. I know my answer."

Patrice Laurent stopped outside the apartment with two officers, slightly out of breath having climbed the stairs. He was worried. The next door opened and a middle aged woman came out into the corridor. "Ah, you are here," she said.

"Madame," Patrice said.

"I've not seen nor heard anything of her for some while now. I was concerned, that's why I called you."

"That is quite right, Madame. So tell me, how long might that be?" He asked.

The woman paused as she thought about it. "A couple of weeks, I think. Usually she comes and goes. That motorbike hasn't been touched either, so I know she's in there."

Patrice nodded and tried the doorbell. Upon getting no answer, he called out while banging on the door with his fist. "Pascale! Are you in there?" Again, no answer. He turned to one of the officers. "We will have to break in."

The man nodded to his colleague and they used a ram to break down the door. Patrice walked briskly from room to room calling out Pascale's name.

"In here," one of the men called from the bedroom.

Patrice followed the sound of the voice and looked down at Pascale. She was inert on the bed. He reached out and checked for a pulse. There was none, yet the body was warm. He lifted an eyelid and the pupil contracted. "How strange."

They tried to revive her, but to no avail. She was somewhere between life and death.

"Better call an ambulance," he ordered.

Pascale woke. The sun shone through the window and lit the room with a glorious warm light that bounced off the sheets and felt like a warm glow on her face. In the en-suite she could hear the water running as Guillaume showered. He would be out soon and she would look upon him and savour the contours of his body, the dark shock of hair and three-day stubble he insisted upon sporting. She imagined holding his firm body close, breathing in the fresh smell of his cologne and feeling the stubble scratching her skin. She looked across at the bedside clock. A little after half past seven. A glorious morning. The start of a new day. A special day.

She remembered this day as if it was yesterday, rather than thirty years ago. They were going to ride south, along the Riviera coast, dropping into Italy. Then down to Tuscany.

She got out of bed and pulled the sheet around her as she walked across to the window. Below in the square she could see the bikes. His Laverda triple and her Harley. Yes, that bike from so long ago. She would get to ride it again. The heady scent of jasmine hung on the air, just as she remembered it.

That evening, following the day's ride, in the light of the dying sun, they would eat a meal, drink some wine and listen to the sound of soft voices, clinking glasses, and the cicadas chirruping on the sultry air, warm still from the heat of the day's sun.

That day was burned into her soul. She could recall every moment because that evening in the quiet of a Tuscan sunset, he proposed. Yes, she could recall every minute even though they had flashed past in the blink of an eye.

But this time was different. This time she would savour every precious second. For this time, the day was going to last for a lifetime.

I'd trade all of my tomorrows, for a single yesterday—"Me and Bobby McGee," Kris Kristofferson.

Dust Mote Meanderings

Wandra Nomad

1-Transition

Carlotta

"Sick up, sick up,
     sick up on the floor orrrr!!!"

"STOP THAT SINGING!" Carlotta took a deep breath and fought for control, even though just the sound of the words chanting forth from this brats' taunting little mouth made her want to puke, and made her seem to smell the odor of vomit just as if it had already happened. Deep breath. *Yuck! Try again.*

"Ricky, stop it *please*. If you keep saying that, then Joey might …" *No. Wrong approach. Don't plant any ideas.* "PLEASE don't keep saying that. Only dogs sick up in the car." *There that shouldn't give any suggestions to present company.*

"Unh unh. Joey does too.
Sick up, sick up,
     sick up on the floor orrrr."

"Riiiicccky! Why do you want to sing that anyway?"

"Cuz when Joey does sick uuuup,
     sick up on the floor orrrr,
  if I don't sing the sick-up song,
     then I'll sick-up some mo orrrrr.
 Sick up, sick up,
     sick up on the floor orrrr!!!"

Carlotta stopped for a red light a mere five blocks from her destination, where she could get rid of this little monster and his brother. She craned around to fix her evil-eye look on the obnoxious mini-twerp, only to see that he was right. Joey *had* . . .

She whirled back around to face the front. Her stomach did flip-flops and she wondered if singing the sick-up song would work for her. Silently chanting "Sick up, sick up, sick up on the floor orrrr!!!" she gripped the wheel, squeezed her eyes tight and concentrated on not parting company with the greasy burger and fries she'd had with these little beasts to fill some of the time. Why, oh why had she chosen today to practice saying "If there's anything I can do..." Ugh! So much for holidays and thankfulness.

Voices seemed to agree with her stupidity asking, "Why"?

Like she knew this would happen? *Who would choose ...!*

When Ricky poked her in the shoulder, she lost her concentration, and spouted forth all over the steering wheel, her lap and even most of the dash. The entire world shrank to wave after wave of streams and clumps spewing forth, until only a bitter burning acid dribbled out along with her dry heaves.

A sharp tapping on her window startled her back to awareness of the car, the chanting brat in the back seat, the sounds of horns blaring and the horrid odor of her own mess added to Joey's.

"Lady, this isn't a parking lot," a voice shouted. "Yah can't just sit here all day. Yah gotta move it." She looked up to find one of the city's 'finest' trying to peer into her window.

In the back seat Ricky got to the window control, lowering it and stuck his head out still chanting,

"Sick up, sick up,

sick up on the floor orrrr!!!

Hello officer. She's sicked up and so's my brother!"

Sick up, sick up,

"Sick up on the floor orrrr!!!"

He snaked his hand along the front window and down until he reached the window controls and held down the button for all four windows. At least some fresher air poured in even if it was laden with the stench of exhaust. Better that than . . .

The baby-faced cop stuck his head into the car and hastily withdrew it.

"Lady, you okay? What's wrong?"

"She sicked-up, just like Joey!

Sick up, sick up,

sick up on ..."

"Ricky! SHUT UP!!!"

"Of course we're not okay! We've got the plague! Gotta get to the quarantine center!" She jerked her foot off the brake and the car lurched forward leaving the jaw gaping young officer behind.

"God damn it! You freaking voices better talk to those lights 'cuz next stop is theirs!"

30

She was astounded that she *did* get every light green until she pulled up to the Royalston Arms.

'Luxury living in the heart of downtown' she read sarcastically.

The doorman came toward her car, to wave her on but seeing Ricky emerge from the back seat, he swerved toward him. Taking Ricky by the hand, he deposited him inside the door to the lobby.

"Now you wait right there, Master Rick."

He returned to the car, reached in for the two small backpacks and the remaining child.

"Oh, oh! New driver – eh? No one warned you that Master Joseph *cannot* eat then ride? Come on little guy." He lifted Joey out, shut the door and headed into the lobby without so much as another glance at the car or its miserable driver.

Carlotta drove off in disgust with all four windows wide open and the A/C going full blast. Ten blocks later she pulled into the car wash and wriggled out of the little car, leaving the keys in it.

Bob

"Inside and out, Bob," she yelled to the attendant then dashed to the ladies room, holding her hand over her mouth even though nothing accompanied the diminishing dry heaves that still wracked her body.

Inside she surveyed the mess and did what she could with paper towels gagging the whole time. She dreaded facing Bob. He always expected 'favors' for his work and she knew he'd want a big pay-off for this one. Fantasy alone might not be enough - even though she considered herself the Queen of Fantasy - just as these skimpy paper towels weren't enough!

Eyeing the door warily – why couldn't it be locked from inside? – she stripped off her slacks. Tailored for the most enhancing effect though they were, even she thought they looked big enough for a whale or an elephant. And why did this miserable facility have to have so many floor length mirrors? Carlotta B. Kidd did *not* enjoy catching glimpses of her billowing rolls of fat.

By fourth grade, when she was already over 5 feet and over 200 lbs, she'd agonized over her name as well. "Carlotta B Kidd" became "A Lotta PIG Kidd" as the other kids taunted. Until she sat on one of them, tore out most of his hair and threatened to remove his ears by twisting them off. Thereafter she never heard it to her face but knew it continued behind her back.

Being the richest kid in the school might have helped if she'd had any social graces. But none ever developed; even before her always too busy parents were killed leaving her to be raised by various virtually emotionless older relatives and indifferent private school staffs.

Get a grip Carlotta! That's the long gone past. At least they left me rich! I'll never have to go through the indignities of finding a job.

While her voluminous trousers dripped water, the pains and rumblings in her lower regions warned her that her bowels wanted to do an encore to her stomach's performance.

Grabbing the spare package of paper towels, she looked over at the stalls for the handicap one, but if one was larger than the others, it must be by only an inch. Holding a stall door half open she reached around to hang her pants on the handbag hook – Damn! She'd left her purse in the car! – She struggled to lower her underwear and collapsed onto the tiny seat scraping her whole left side on the toilet paper dispenser.

Her knees extended too far and were too wide to allow her to close the door of the cubicle. Who did they think had knees that could fit in the two-inch space between the john and the door and then try opening and shutting it? The freaking door should open outward! She ought to sue the sons of bitches! But that would require putting a spotlight on her gargantuan size in a courtroom.

She grimaced as the first of several lengthy butt-belches erupted from her in a cacophony of increasing odor and volume. She writhed around to position her elbow to push the flush lever behind her after each bout, wondering how so much odor could waft its way to her nostrils when she seemed to so thoroughly seal off the space below. And forget that crap about dogs don't smell their own stink. Maybe dogs don't but that sure didn't work for Carlotta. The pains in her abdomen were accompanied by excess secretions of saliva and dry heaves wracked her again.

Stupid Bob opened the outer door just enough for his voice to enter and called,

"Are you okay in there?"

Sound effects from the loudest, longest, most liquid anal eruption yet and agonized retching noises were all he got for an answer and he made a hasty retreat.

That was when the disembodied voices began again. She ignored them.

"Why does she stay?"

"That species thinks they have no choice."

"Why not?"

"They believe sensation, intellect and mass require interconnection. So, for them, they do."

"But why do they insist on so *much* mass and emotion?"

"They seem to think they need mass to carry the intellect."

"But they miniaturize what they call artificial intelligence."

"Yes, but they haven't yet tried to apply the same idea to themselves."

"Why don't we just change them?"

"You know the rules. Encouragement not interference."

"Yes, but it seems an ineffective way to exist. I want to end this."

"You know the rules. You have to finish the course. So return."

"But in there I have all the sensations she does."

"That's the point. To become a scholar of galactic species, you must sample them."

"But …"

"Oh SHUT UP!" Carlotta screamed! And the voices did, but she was aware that the sense of having a 'watcher' inside her mind had returned. For weeks now she'd been plagued by one or the other.

Carlotta eventually sidled out of the restroom, hoping she could avoid Bob for once. No luck! There he was leaning against the wall beside the door.

"Hey Lotta, you owe me big time."

"Yeah, well not today, I'm sick and I'm late."

"How about I come by your house later?" He waggled his eyes at her.

How could the creep even think she might be interested? Thank God, she'd never given him her address.

"Oh, I don't think so, I probably won't be there."

He followed her to her car. After she crammed herself in she began groping through her purse, to pay him.

"Oh, I almost forgot." He reached into his pocket and pulled out her wallet. "You left this just sitting there, so I thought I should protect it for you. And you can just sign this." He extended an already swiped credit card slip.

Grrrr, what a sleaze, yet in spite of herself she began to weave a fantasy. My, what she could do with this creep. He did seem to love the fantasies she could weave. Would he love 'payback' ones?

She belched and an acrid burning in her throat might have caused a resumption of the vomiting except there was nothing left. After a couple of gags she recovered.

"What's wrong with you?" Bob actually sounded concerned.

"They think it's the plague. I have to get to the Quarantine Center."

Bob backed away, "The plague? But people don't get the plague anymore – do they? What Quarantine Center? I never heard of it."

"Whoops. Yeah, best kept secret. Only a few cases around anymore so they only tell you about the Quarantine Center if they think you need it. To avoid public panic, you know?" Bob was turning from white to colorless.

She drove off before he could respond and managed not to burst into laughter until she rounded the corner.

"Just kidding around, Bob!" said the 'Queen of Fantasy' laughing.

That might even keep Bob from showing up on her doorstep. However, as long as he never appeared at her door, fantasies of what she might do to and with him if he did show up could entertain her for weeks. And Carlotta definitely tended to prefer her sexual fantasies to her sexual realities. Pleasing though Bob's imagined gropings and thrustings might be, titillating though the fantasy of being caught at it was, their greatest thrill was to fuel new fantasies.

Now Bob had her address she'd have to move and find a new car wash. Oh well, she was beginning to tire of Bob anyway. If not for the fun idea of stirring up his germ phobia, she'd never go back there. But, Carlotta decided, she just had to see how much of a rise she'd gotten out of him.

There was another whole vein of mental machinations to be tapped. Sickness and contagion fantasies could be just as potent as sexual ones; and could be played out in real life more often, always with her favorite pun ending – 'just kidding around'.

When life gives you lemons, you make lemonade, when life names you Kidd you do a lot of kidding!

Carlotta

Carlotta put fantasy fun and games out of her mind for the moment and turned her thoughts to the voices. Now there was a consideration; fantasy or real? Is reality a fantasy? Or is fantasy the true reality? That was a question that Carlotta, the self-proclaimed 'Queen of Fantasy', was grappling with.

Shunned and ridiculed in childhood due to her enormous size she'd developed minuscule social skills, so she'd turned inward and mastered fantasy to a fine-tuned skill. Name a topic, Carlotta could be in a world-class fantasy in seconds, not that anyone else ever knew – or cared – except Bob. Some people could create songs or jingles instantly on demand but Carlotta chose to be the 'Queen of Fantasy'.

Sexual fantasies were easy. Carlotta didn't need sex toys, alcohol, drugs, sexy outfits, scents, candles, aphrodisiacs or partners. All she needed was to turn on her mind and let it go.

Overhearing a chance phrase in passing could light the fire. She once heard some guys talking. One said, "It was so weird. She'd let me do anything except kiss her." Wham! Carlotta was off and running with it. Just imagine! … And she did.

Once she read about a pregnancy happening because the girl didn't think anything could happen if she kept her bathing suit on. Wham! Just imagine … Again, Carlotta was off and running with it.

Another chance comment, "She said he never touched her. He just kept telling her things he was going to do but kept his hands always at least a half inch away from her." Wham!

Putting people 'in their place' fantasies were another favorite. These she often worked on until they were polished nuggets and then she tried them out in real life. Like today's Quarantine Center. Fantasies of spreading rumors of sickness, doom and disaster were good for laughs. And were soooo fun to use in real life. Sometimes she was the savior but more often, she was gaining her revenge on all who had ever ridiculed her. There were endless opportunities to have the scumbags of her life groveling at her feet, their destiny in Carlotta's hands.

Another favorite category was, 'been there, done that'. Reading was very real to her. Someone might ask "Did you read the book or see the movie?" and Carlotta would answer "Yes." not be sure which she'd done.

Even more so were her fantasies about places and events she'd never been to. Some were so profound she began to have trouble distinguishing them from reality. Not in the 'crazy' sense, but in the way they were as powerful in memory as actual trips she'd taken. And when a fantasy series culminated in a trip to that location, she often experienced déjà vu - feeling sure she had been there before.

Yes, Carlotta had become fantasizer extraordinaire. Then she began fantasizing about fantasy. Could you really make a trip to the twilight zone via fantasy? Was fantasy a way to enter alternative realities? Or even a way to tour the universe. What if …? What about dreams? What about near death experiences? Could fantasy be akin to out of body experience? Was all of this something one could gain conscious control over?

Then came the voices. She didn't think they were distortions of a disordered mind. She also did not seem to hear them *in* her head. They always seemed a foot or two from her head and to be conjecturing *about* her. She wished now she'd listened better today. But they had a nasty little habit of coming when she was distressed or too distracted to attend to them well.

As she drove, Carlotta pondered the problem of Bob. She couldn't bear the thought of him showing up at her door. Fantasy was great but *reality*? Well *that* had a displeasing habit of being not so great. Perhaps she'd go to a hotel and live the life of luxury until she could get moved. She did have her name on the list for those nice new apartments about ready to open across town.

A plan began to formulate and soon Carlotta's spirits were as high as the clouds drifting overhead and her thoughts were as light. Yes! Bob and she never crossed paths except at the car wash. She'd disappear and when she reappeared, she'd tell him she'd been in the quarantine center. And YES! She'd tell him the incubation period was however long she'd been gone – ah but that's with preventative treatment – twice that long without it. Yes, she began embellishing it with the most joyful details. Bob your time to pay up is coming – just when you'll least expect it.

But back to the voices; she found them most unsettling. She knew all her other plots and fantasies were her own. With the voices she just wasn't sure. It was annoyingly aggravating that she couldn't turn them on and off like she could everything else. Since she could not control them maybe she should consider what they said.

"Oh darn!" Paying no attention to her driving Carlotta suddenly realized she was turning into her street. "Nope! No way! That slimy creep Bob has my address now!"

She took the next side street to get out of there. For tonight at least, she'd have to go somewhere he couldn't find her. She could go clear out of her apartment sometime she was sure Bob was at work. After stopping at Walmart to pick up some sleepwear and a change of clothes she searched for a place for the night. She remembered a ritzy looking place outside of town and headed there.

When she saw that it had an out of sight parking lot she decided it was perfect and booked a comfortable suite for a month and settled in. Being careful she paid cash and used a fake name.

Voices

"Now!" she thought, "it is time to figure out these darned voices. All right you voices! Talk to me now so I can figure this out!"

She folded her arms and waited – and waited. Nothing!

She tried again – but still nothing! How aggravating!

Though irritated maybe she could recreate what she'd heard. Telling herself to stay calm, she tried to focus on just the voices she heard today. It wasn't easy to keep focused on that and not the other disturbing events at the time. Her stomach lurched at the memory.

Why did they always come when she was too upset to pay full attention? And why until today did they seem related enough to the situation at hand to be brushed aside? But not today. She had a feeling that today's bit was more about *her* not about the situation. Had they all been that way? Why couldn't she recall? And why did she so often get the feeling of a 'watcher' lurking in her brain?

As she pondered her stomach growled. "Damn! That's not 'lurching' that's hunger!" Well it *had* been several hours since her stomach emptied and she'd not eaten since. She ordered room service complete with everything that might appeal, with ample desserts too. After polishing off much of it she fell asleep.

Carlotta was floating. She had no idea where she was or how it happened but she was floating. Floating, floating, floating!

How lovely she thought, and tried to figure out where she was.

"She did it!" cried a voice.

"Not really," replied another. "She must be able to do it when in her conscious state."

Huh? Do they mean me? Carlotta pondered.

She did just seem to be drifting in the air. She tried to look around but couldn't really turn very well.

"And she must gain control," added the second voice.

Carlotta awoke with a start. *Voices in her room!*

Who was with her! Had that creep Bob found her? How could he?

After a panicky deep breath she decided there was no one there. But she had heard the voices! What had they said?

She struggled to recall. Do what? Control what?

After a while she went back to sleep and dreamed of floating free of her body and worries. During this dream she found she could not actually 'move' or redirect herself but if she fantasized being at specific spot in the room sometimes she would suddenly be there.

When she woke, Carlotta felt that was her best sleep ever and was eager to see if she would have that tantalizing dream again.

Over the next few nights she did and liked it so much that she began going to bed earlier, getting up later. And trying to take day time naps but found herself too rested for naps. After several days she sometimes began to have the same feeling if she just closed her eyes and thought hard about it. Soon she was floating whenever she tried. She thought of her floating as being like a dust mote.

Just when she was getting to love this new fantasy life the voices began again. Now they seemed to talking to her rather than about her.

"Where have you been?" she asked, not expecting a reply.

"You didn't need us once you began."

Startled, Carlotta thought "Well that seems rather cryptic."

But she'd gotten a direct answer, of sorts, from one of the voices! Excited she tried again.

"Why are you back now?"

"We are not back because we never left. We have been watching."

Creepy!

"Sooooo why are you talking to me now?"

"It is time for you to be aware of your purpose."

"And just what might that purpose be?"

"You make the transition then will aid with the transition of your kind."

Carlotta felt bewildered so just raised an eyebrow and waited for the voice to go on. When that didn't happen she asked, "What transition?"

"To what you call dust mote."

"Huh? Wha – Why? How?" *Damn! I sound like '20 Questions' she thought.*

"Yes," the second voice agreed.

Shit! They can read my thoughts! "Explain!" Carlotta demanded.

"Your planet can no longer support an intelligent species so dependent on mass."

"Huh?"

"Your kind destroys the planet. You will aid your kind with transition."

"What transition?"

"As you are doing."

"Ummmm – you mean convert the human race into ummm, floating dust motes?" Carlotta scoffed.

"Yes."

"Yeah ri - ight! And just how will I be able to do that?"

"You will figure it out."

"Huh? No way! I don't even know what you've done!"

"You will figure it out. It is time for us to leave."

"But – why *me*?"

"Your mind was ready."

"Wait! What …? How?"

"As we have done with you."

"But you were talking about non-interference."

"The rules are less confining for one's own kind."

"So just what are these *rules*?"

"We don't know yours, but you will figure it out."

Carlotta suddenly realized she was floating and tried to go back to her body. She couldn't. *I can't find my body! I can't even SEE my body!*

"Where's my body?" she screamed, panic increasing with each word!

"Gone. Body no longer needed."

"WHAT?" Anger replaced her panic as Carlotta screamed, "Hey it was a lousy body to get stuck with but it was *mine* and I want it. Where is it?"

"Gone. Body no longer needed."

"Well it is mine! I want it! Bring it back!"

"Not possible. Molecules dispersed."

"Molecu … What the … Hey wait a minute! What if I refuse to do what you say?"

"Then yours will be a very solitary existence. It is time for us to go."

"Go where?"

"To help others like you, around your galaxy."

Galaxy! "Why?"

"Only then can we return to our home. It is time for us to go."

"Where are you from?"

"Outside of your galaxy. It is time for us to go."

"Wait! Are you the voices I've been hearing?"

"Yes. It is time…"

"And the – the – uh 'watcher' I was feeling in my brain?" Carlotta interrupted.

"Yes. It is time for us to go."

"No! Wait! Why don't you *aid* this transition?"

"Our powers are restricted away from our galaxy."

"What's that supposed to mean?"

"We can only prime suitable – ummm – triggers – like you. Now, it is time for us to go."

"Wait! I have more questions."

There was no reply. Carlotta raged and waited but there was only silence.

"Shit!"

After several minutes passed she concentrated on being more mobile in order to search the room for the voices. She was pretty sure she had moved around in her dreams but now she seemed only able to 'float'.

She neither saw nor heard the voices again. She tried again and again to return to her body. She could not, it just wasn't there.

Carlotta suddenly became aware that she'd been transitioned into a dust mote

– a dust mote with a *mission*.

2 - Mission

Carlotta

So I'm nothing more than a dust mote now! With a mission! Shit!!!

Carlotta did not like being told what to do. Further she still didn't know 'how' she could accomplish such a mission.

Jeez! You'd think a transformation that got rid of my body would make life easier but what good is it if I can't move from this spot?"

She got no answer. Listen though she might, the only 'voice' Carlotta heard in her head now was her own memory of a 'voice' saying. "You will figure it out."

Yeah ri-ight!! Shouldn't you have taught me? Or at least have guided me?

Again there was no answer.

Well I haven't figured it out!

Fighting panic again, instead of trying to navigate around the room, she tried instead to *resist* the floating. She imagined herself remaining in one spot.

Wow! This is easier. And it is progress – sort of!

However, being able to float or not float wasn't getting her anywhere.

What else had those other voices said?

"Your mind was ready."

Well it doesn't seem very 'ready' to me!

Time seemed to have little meaning now but she felt certain that a lot of it had passed. Carlotta, if she *was* still Carlotta, was startled by the hotel room door opening. She felt helpless as she saw her few things being removed from the room and listened to two maids chatting as they cleaned the room.

"What became of the woman who was in here?"

"Dunno, but she must have been a giant judging by these clothes she left behind."

Hey you bitch! That's not nice! Carlotta was furious.

The maid who'd insulted Carlotta spun around and asked the other one, "What did you say? What did you call me?"

"Nothing! I didn't say anything," answered the other maid.

"Well someone did! It *wasn't* your voice but we're the only ones here! Didn't you hear it?"

"I heard something, like a whisper, but it was not me. Maybe it was the A/C kicking on."

She gave her companion a shrug.

"I'm going to take this laundry and these dirty dishes out. How long has she been gone? The left-over food on these dishes is either dried out like a brick or buried knee deep in mold."

"Dunno – all I know is she prepaid for a month but was only seen once after she checked in. She left strict orders to not be disturbed for anything! So there was no housekeeping or anything."

"Nothing? No one saw her? Now she's just vanished?"

"A waiter saw her once when she ordered room service, enough for an army so I heard. No wonder she was so huge!" she mused to the disappearing back of the other maid.

Shut up you bitch!

"Okay! Okay! But you shouldn't be monitoring rooms during cleaning." The maid looked around for a camera or listening device. There didn't seem to be one but they were clever at hiding them these days.

That's not someone monitoring you. It's me and it's me you are badmouthing so you had better shape up or I'll transition you!

"What the …? Do what?" Grabbing the last items needing to be removed from the room the maid left, closing the door with an uneasy backward glance.

Alone again Carlotta pondered what had happened.

Hmmmmm can't move around but I can project my' voice' well enough. I guess that's something. Maybe I should have transitioned her just for some company.

She waited to find out what would happen when this room would have new 'guests' – *her* guests to experiment with she hoped. Her chance to begin her mission.

But for now I gotta figure out how to get around. No arms! No legs! How am I supposed to move?! There must be a way to move around. *'They' seemed to – even around a galaxy – or more it sounded like. So I should be able to.*

Searching her memory, all Carlotta came up with was 'you will figure it out'. *It seems like I moved around when they were here? How? No, I guess I only moved around when I had a body. So, how did they do it? Hmmmm no eyes – but I can see, no ears – but I can hear, no mouth – but I can 'talk'. Interesting! I don't THINK about seeing or hearing or talking – but I do all of them.*

How did she move around when they were here? Hmm-mm then she was asleep – dreaming, and moving around without trying. Then – if she 'thought' about her body she'd be back in it. But that doesn't work now. "Body gone. Body no longer needed!" they'd said.

Can I sleep now? How long have I been awake? Time seemed meaningless. And though she tried over and over Carlotta seemed unable to fall asleep.

Before she'd figured out anything, Carlotta was startled by the flurry of a man checking into the room. *This could prove interesting.*

He seemed to have a limitless amount of alcohol with him and to drink it constantly. Carlotta visualized herself viewing him from several areas of the room and was surprised that it happened. Pondering that at length, she finally realized that it worked when she fantasized or just saw herself there it happened, but not when she just 'thought' about it or 'tried' to do it. After experimenting several times, she felt assured she could move around the room when and where she wanted.

That must be what 'they' meant about my mind being 'ready'. So the 'Queen of Fantasy' reigns supreme! Carlotta smiled.

Well, damn! That's rather unsporting of you!

While Carlotta B Kidd, the self-proclaimed Queen of Fantasy, who now seemed caught in this 'unreal' situation, had been figuring out how to navigate around this room, the drunk, who unknowingly shared the room with her, had quietly fallen into a stuporous sleep.

Pondering her situation, she wondered if she actually *was* caught in a very elaborate fantasy. If so, was this a fantasy of her own weaving? *But how could it be? Why would I ever dream up something this weird?*

Recently, well, since time seemed to be losing meaning she thought it was recent, her life had dramatically changed. From a person of overly abundant flesh and bone she seemed to have been prodded, by disembodied voices, into 'transitioning' into seemingly pure energy with consciousness, in a mass about the size of a dust mote.

Or was this all one of her own elaborate fantasies taking on a life of its own? *But how could it be? Why would I ever fantasize something like this?* That was the question she kept repeating.

If this was as 'real' as it seemed to be, having figured out how to navigate, the next step in her 'mission' would seem to be to aid others in making the same sort of transition. The only unhelpful guidance given to her by those blasted voices was, 'you will figure it out.' But now her only guinea pig had fallen asleep and she was very leery of waking a drunk.

Well, much of my communication with the voices was in my dreams. But do I really want to try to enter the dreams of a drunk. Can I even do that? Can I enter someone's dream?

Carlotta tried to look at this question from all possible perspectives but finally just decided *I won't know unless I try*.

Focusing on the sleeping man she visualized herself creeping slowly into his brain. *Ugh! Kinda creepy!* Before she was fully immersed she met a chorus of voices challenging her.

"Who the heck are you?"

"Where'd you come from?"

"What're yah doin' here?"

"Whadda ya want?"

"Get out!"

"Leave us alone!"

"Go away!"

Carlotta quickly withdrew. *Phew! Kinda crowded in there!*

She was startled by the drunk sitting up and clutching his head.

"Will the whole damn bunch of yez just SHUT UP?! I'm sick of hearing yer constant bickering!"

A quick look around assured Carlotta that they were alone in the room.

But apparently this man is not alone in his head.

Since he seemed to be awake she decided to speak to him.

What was all that? she asked.

"Oh so now one of yez wants to be pretend to be outside my head? Well I don't care, inside or outside, just shut up – all of yez!"

I just want to help ...

"I said SHUT UP! None of yez has evah wanted to help anyone. All yez do iz torture a guy!"

Why don't you leave them?

"Yer think thas eashy? Look at you shtill bugging me afta I keep telling yer to SHUT THE HELL UP!"

Carlotta figured she was not experienced enough to handle the situation so kept silent while she tried to think what to do.

I better find someone else. Maybe I can slip out too when he leaves this room.

Having thought she finally had a chance to give her 'mission' a try, it was quite disheartening to be rejected on her first attempt. She wasn't exactly in a crowd where she could pick and choose who to practice with.

She mentally sighed. *Maybe when that door opens again I can slip out.*

Waiting wasn't easy for Carlotta but what else could she do?

But ... wait, the voices left me without opening a door. Maybe I should try it!

She tried to think how the hallway and the outside of the door had looked.

Ri-ight! Like I was paying attention! Anyway aren't hotel hallways sort of generic?

She tried visualizing a generic hallway. Nothing. She didn't dare fantasize too specifically for fear of ending up somewhere she didn't know and not know how to get back.

All she could clearly remember of the hotel was the reception area and the dippy clerk who'd checked her in. There was an odd shaped scratch on the counter that she had noticed.

That's pretty far from this room!

She wondered if she could go that far. If she could even manage to leave this room at all! Well they had mentioned galaxies.

So why not give it a try?

She mentally closed her eyes and visualized the scratch on the counter from when she was checking in.

Poof!

Carlotta and Kirk

There she was in the reception area with no one around except a different bored looking clerk focused on a computer. From the sounds it seemed he was playing a game.

Must be a nice job if you can just sit there and play games!

The clerk looked around but saw no one and resumed his game.

You get paid to do that or are you the owner's kid?

This time the clerk stood up and approached the counter to look over it.

"Who said that?" he asked. "Where are you?"

I did but don't worry you can't see me. No one can.

"What kind of gimmick is this?"

No gimmick, I just came to offer you a more interesting life.

"Sure! Try to sell me some kinda voice projection equipment that I know I can't afford! So take your gimmicks and sales pitch somewhere else."

No gimmicks and no sales pitch – this is something you have to do yourself.

"Well I can't afford your self-help books or tapes or whatever you're selling."

Can you imagine a better life for yourself?

"Sure and it wouldn't be here. This is just a temporary rest stop to get a few bucks to move on with."

Can you imagine leaving your body?

"So you peddling some kind of fake 'out of body' shit?"

Fake? No, but out of body? Yes.

"Whadda yah mean? Show yourself and we can talk more."

"I can't do that. But I can help you transition to a different existence."

"How?"

Can you visualize leaving your body and floating up to the ceiling?

"This is some weird gimmick? OK. I'm bored here so I'll play along."

Carlotta waited then asked, *are you floating at the ceiling?*

"Not likely but the idea of floating could be fun, right?"

Sure but you have to do more than have the 'idea of it'. Can you visualize it? See it? Be it?

"OK. Hey! Yeah! I can see it! Oh whoops I opened my eyes and now I'm right down here where I've been all along."

Well that's a good start. Why don't you try again and really concentrate on staying up near the ceiling while your body stays down below.

"OK. Hey this is neat! How do you do it? Oh whoops – back down here again."

I don't do it. You do. Want to try again?

"Sure but maybe I should sit down so I won't fall and get hurt while I'm out of my body" he said with a chuckle.

Good idea.

"Hey! This is cool! How do you do it?"

I told you, I don't. You do it with your mind.

"I could really get 'into' this – like full-time – yah know."

If you want to, you can. There's just one condition.

"Ri-ight I knew there'd be a catch! What do I have to buy and how much is it?"

Nothing. Just make a promise. Once you can do this on your own you have to help other people to do the same.

"That's IT?"

Yup.

"OK, sure."

OK, try again but this time talk to me from up there.

"Ummm OK. Hey! I'm up here but where are you? I've yet to see you."

That's good!

"Oh! Shucks now I'm down here again."

Keep practicing and soon you won't need that body anymore.

"Great! I like this." came his voice from the ceiling. "But if I get good at it I can't just leave my body sitting around! How do I handle that?"

It will be taken care of.

"How?"

You will figure it out.

"OK. Sure, but you said I have to help others do this – how?"

You will figure it out.

Carlotta decided to leave him to it. Just as she was about to visualize herself elsewhere the guy's body disappeared.

Gulp! That was pretty fast!

"Hey! Where's my body? I can't find it!"

You no longer need a body.

"What! That wasn't something I bargained for!"

Yes you did.

"Yeah? When?"

When you asked for full-time basis.

Amazed that the clerk had transitioned so fast, Carlotta quickly visualized herself back in the hotel room with the drunk. She couldn't think where else to go in a hurry.

That's creepy! How'd he make the transition so quickly? Those voices bugged me for weeks before they transitioned me! And how did I know to say some of those things?

After considerable thought she decided the voices must have pre-programmed her unconscious with a manual or something.

She began wondering about the poor guy in the office. He's probably as confused and feeling even more helpless than she had. And she wondered how his boss or others would react to his abrupt disappearance. She could just 'see' him confused and struggling to understand and being stuck on the ceiling in the reception area. That put her back there.

Are you still here?

"Yeah but where have the heck have you been? That was a pretty mean trick to stick me up here and leave me dangling." In his now diminishing panic and relief to hear her voice again, he giggled.

You transitioned so fast it alarmed me. This is my first try. It took weeks for the voices to transition me.

"What IS going on here?" His voice was full of bewilderment and resurfacing panic.

With a loud sigh, Carlotta said, *I'll explain. That's what I came back for. Just calm down and listen.*

She told him everything she could remember of her encounters with the voices.

He listened quietly except to exclaim, "Another galaxy, wow!" and "Yeah humans cause a lot of damage to the planet."

When she finished he said, "So I can go anywhere just by 'seeing' myself there. So far all I've really tried to see is my body 'cuz I don't like the idea of being stuck up here the rest of my life. But that didn't work. I'm trying it now. Oh wow it works! Now I'm on the counter!"

Me too.

After a pause he said, "Strange, everything that I was wearing is also gone but my tablet is still there on the desk. Guess I won't be needing it. Like how would I even carry it around," he giggled again. "Hey is this how it was with you?"

Yeah, about the same. When they cleared out the hotel room my clothes and stuff were still there.

"Room? Where were you?"

In a room here.

"What's your name?"

When she told him, he sounded disappointed. "Oh, I thought you might be the lady who went missing here. That wasn't her name though. But hey! I think that's the name on the registration of the car that was abandoned here!"

Yeah, that was me! What happened with my car?

"It was impounded as 'abandoned' and put in storage somewhere. But it wasn't your name."

Oh, that. I was avoiding someone so I signed in with a fake name.

"So it was you that disappeared here?"

Literally! Ummm – How will the hotel react to another disappearance?

"Another? Oh, you mean me! Dunno but they'll probably just think I 'moved on' without telling them. I was pretty lucky to get this job. I wandered in when my boss was desperate for someone to be in here for this graveyard shift – the shift when nothing ever happens – until now."

What about your family and friends? Won't they wonder where you are?

"I don't know of any who'd miss me." said Kirk. "Soooooo, what is it we are supposed to do?"

We are supposed to help other people to 'transition' like we have.

"But how?"

They didn't give me a manual! I guess they just expect us to figure it out. And I did manage it with you by sort of copying what they did with me.

"Okaaay. But I think we ought to give them – ummm – the new dust motes – give them more guidance than we got."

Agreed.

It did seem to Carlotta like the voices had left her with much to be desired. But here they were and it certainly would be a lonely existence if they didn't do as the 'voices' expected.

As Carlotta and Kirk were discussing the 'mission' thrust upon them by disembodied voices, a buzzer sounded and the outer door of the reception area opened.

"Hey kid?

My boss. Kirk thought to Carlotta.

"Kirk? Where are you? Time to go. Hey! Where are you, kid?"

Carlotta silently messaged the clerk *I'll get this.*

She quickly entered the boss's mind and planted a thought that came out of his mouth, "Damned drifter! Probably 'drifted on' without bothering to let me know!" he shrugged. "Funny he didn't wait to get paid though! Strange that he left his highfalutin phone behind too. Seemed like he couldn't breathe without that thing."

Let's get out of here. Ummm – let's both go to the top of that tall light in the parking lot.

"Oh that worked great!"

Kirk?

"Yeah I'm Kirk or was."

So, now he thinks you're a drifter. Does that work for you?

"Sure. I guess I sort of am or was a drifter – a fun-loving drifter. Which is why I doubt anyone will miss me. What about you?"

Carlotta. I'm not a 'drifter' but I can't think of anyone who might notice that I'm missing. The few people who know – er knew me – knew I was about to move, soooo…

"So, Carlotta, what IS a dust mote?" Kirk asked.

Huh? I thought that was common knowledge!

"Guess I'm not common enough." Kirk chuckled.

Well, you know when the sun is streaming in a window you can see little specks of dust floating in the air? Those are often called dust motes.

"Dust? So we are dust? And we do have mass? Even if tiny?"

I don't know. That was just a term that came to my mind.

"Why? Could you see them?"

I don't know. Well maybe there were dust motes in the room.

"Can you see me?"

I don't know. I haven't tried.

"The sun's up. Let's go back inside, into some sunlight and see what happens. And then come back here."

Back outside Kirk asked, "Well did you see me?"

I'm not sure. I saw some dust motes but I don't know if one of them was you. Did you see me?

"Same here. But I bet two of those were us!"

Possibly.

"Yah know, being in sunshine or not seems to make no difference to us. What effect does bad weather have on us?"

I guess we will have to wait and find out.

"Yeah. Umm ... No! I'm going to see what happens now! I'll jump in that fountain over there! That'll be like rain."

Be careful! Kirk! Where are you?

"In the fountain."

And?

"Nothing! Yah know – I didn't feel any difference being inside in the A/C than out here in the heat either. So maybe weather has no effect on us. But I guess that makes sense."

Why?

"Well if 'they' travel though space or outer space – ummmm from other galaxies, yah know? – I doubt the elements have much effect on them. Sort of like light waves or radio signals maybe."

That does make sense. Carlotta almost hated having to give this rambunctious 'youngster' that much credit. But she supposed that his quick imagination is what allowed him to make such a quick transition.

"Do you think all dust motes are really from outer space or at least from beyond our galaxy?"

I doubt it – why would droves of them come here?

"Good point. But if some of them are then maybe we also can travel to other galaxies."

Well maybe but I don't think I'll try that anytime soon.

"I wonder what will happen if we try to travel through time."

Let's hold that off for another time too.

"Jeez, have you no sense of adventure?"

I just prefer to go slow. You may be too adventurous!

"Yeah *you'd* think like that!"

For now let's stick with this planet and this time.

"Ok – for now – but what is it we are supposed to do and how?"

Help other people transition like was done to us.

"Okaaaay?"

But I think we have to go slow and be careful until we know what the effects are. We can't just make heaps of people disappear. Other people would notice – friends, families, and others.

"I suppose. Look! There's a dog! Do you think it would work on him?"

I don't know – but...

"I'm gonna try!"

Carlotta sighed and waited. Soon Kirk giggled before he spoke.

"Didn't work! Either he's dumb or I don't speak 'dog' good enough."

Did you really think that would work?

"Well we have to try things to see what works – don't we? How else can we figure this out?"

I suppose.

"How about other languages?"

I don't know. Do you speak any?

"Just a tad bit of several, from my travels. You?"

Just a tiny bit of school book French and German.

"How are we supposed to 'hook' people who don't speak our language?"

We'll just have to figure it out as we go along. Could we just take it slow?

"Why? What's wrong with exploring? You just have no sense of adventure."

And you seem to have an overabundance of it!

"Huh! Maybe we should go our own ways and compare notes later."

Good idea! Carlotta was tired of his exuberance.

"How about if we meet at the clock tower in town at noon everyday?"

How will we know the time? I don't even know what time it is now!

"That's why I figured we should meet at the clock tower - we can look to see the time. In case either of us goofs, let's try to be there every day at noon for now – OK?"

Fine!

"OK! I'm off to see the world! I'll see –er – hear you tomorrow."

Fine! Carlotta sighed in relief. *This effervescent young man sure takes a different approach to things.*

3 - Explorations

Carlotta and Bob

Kirk – you here?

Several times Carlotta had come to this clock tower to meet Kirk – who had an annoying habit of not showing up.

"Carlotta?" a voice called but it wasn't Kirk.

Bob? What are you doing here? This was the first time anyone had answered her. In her explorations in the last few days she had gone to check on Bob at the car wash a few times but he was never there.

"Surprise!"

But HOW - WHO?

"A voice, errr guy, errr dust mote, called Kirk. Said he keeps missing you here but remembered you mentioning a car wash and visited a few looking for 'Bob' –and Voila!"

But…!

"He thought you might get lonely or need help so he asked me to stop by here now and then, too."

So you let him 'transition' you?

"Let him? Practically begged him you mean!"

Why?

"You didn't think working at a car wash was the most scintillating of jobs did you?"

Ummmm – well not really. When did you transition?

"A few days ago, just about quitting time. Then I quit for good!" he laughed.

53

"Well – it is good to have company, I guess. Did he explain the mission to you?"

"Of course. How many transitions have you aided Lotta? It's been what – about a week since he left you?"

She didn't want to discourage him – or maybe she did.

Oh, I usually manage 1 or sometimes 2 a day. I guess – about 10.

"In about a week?"

Yes. She said proudly.

"Why not more?"

What! Well – it takes a while to locate people who won't be missed. Then it usually takes quite a while to sway them.

"Why worry about them being missed?"

Don't you think that would be tough on friends, families, etc.

"Well just transition them too?"

Huh!

"Lotta, where do you find these 'no one will miss them' ones you transition?"

In a lot of 'out of the way' places. I've been focusing on the homeless.

"And no one else around them ever got curious?"

I try to find them alone. Once another homeless guy I didn't know was there and asked what I was doing. So I told him to wait and then helped him to transition too.

"So you only do one at a time?"

Of course! Why?

"Well isn't 'one at a time' pretty slow?"

Sure but ... Well ... How many have you done Bob?

"I wasn't counting but a few hundred or so."

In a few days? Carlotta's voice dripped sarcasm and disbelief.

"Ummm yeah!"

How'd you manage that?

"Groups. Didn't Kirk explain to you how to do groups?"

Kirk! No way! I haven't heard a thing from that drifter since we went our separate ways!

"Oh! Sorry."

So, Bob how do you transition a group?

"Well it is pretty simple – if the people you are focused on are interested then you make sure they are touching each other then – Voila! – Too bad Kirk didn't fully train you!"

54

Train me? Kirk? You gotta be kidding!

"Well yeah. It seems unfair to transition someone and not give then the low down."

But Kirk did NOT transition me!

"Really?"

Is that what Kirk told you?

"No. I just thought since he knew you too … Well, he didn't really tell me anything about you except to ask me to come by here to look for you"

Yeah! Well you got it backwards!

"So you transitioned him?"

Uh-huh!

"So why don't you know about doing groups? One-by-one seems so slow and cumbersome."

Dunno!

"And who trained Kirk? He seems like a real expert on all this."

Dunno!

They both fell silent – each pursuing their own train of thought. Bob was the first to speak.

"Lotta, I feel like finding a group or two to transition now. With so many people on earth it seems like we should keep working."

Maybe I'll tag along to see how you do a group. Carlotta's voice still dripped with disbelief.

"OK. But let me just tell you first so you'll understand more."

I'm listening.

"First find a group."

Of course!

"Good places to look are schools, sports events, theaters and things like that. Then you prime them to be receptive."

Uh – 'prime' them – how?

"Well you just go in their minds and sort of suggest that they want a different existence."

You what? How do you do that for God's sake!

"Haven't you ever influenced anyone's thoughts?" Bob thought about the fantasies she used to spin for him. "I mean as a dust mote?"

Of course not! Errr well – maybe a little bit. When Kirk had just changed someone, his boss, came looking for him and I kinda planted a thought for the guy to believe Kirk was a drifter. He kinda thought that anyway but I helped make it stronger.

"Exactly! So you do already know how to do it."

I guess...

"Same with a group. Haven't you noticed most people dream of a different life?"

Well not really. Carlotta had never really paid much attention to the inner life of others.

"Well most people do. So you reinforce the idea that they each wish to have a less cumbersome life. Or a more meaningful one, or a healthier one, or ... whatever fits the situation. Then you have them hold hands ...

Hold hands?

"... or in some way touch one another and visualize that. And Voila! Actually I am not sure they 'have' to even be touching."

But – well – isn't the sudden disappearance of a whole group noticed?

"Well yeah. In fact the media are already reporting on inexplicable large group disappearances around the world."

And isn't that – well kinda deceitful?

"Not really – anyone who objects or just doesn't have a dream is allowed to opt out or leave. We just erase it for them."

Erase it!?

"Make it so they don't remember even being there. Let's go give it a try. I think there's a game at the stadium today."

The stadium! That would be hundreds of people! Or thousands! You can do that many at once?

"I think so. We're sort of like mental radios I guess. Let's go see what happens."

You think! But you don't know?

"True but everything I've tried so far has worked."

I doubt I'd be much help if it didn't go well. I'd rather start with something smaller.

"Fine how about a ..."

Actually I think I'd rather just practice on my own. I ...

They heard laughter.

"That's Carlotta for you! No sense of adventure!" another voice chortled.

Carlotta was NOT amused.

Kirk, Bob and Carlotta

Kirk! You finally decided to grace me with a visit!

"I kept missing you here! Besides, I've been busy." Kirk replied. "Let me show you."

Kirk had left eager to explore the world. He'd also felt pity for Carlotta. To have such a wonderful gift and to be so reluctant to explore with it seemed sad to him.

For a complete change of mood when he left Carlotta he decided to try to go to Thailand first. He'd loved his first visit there and was always longing to return. He could easily visualize a gorgeous white temple with a steep red roof and gold trim. He abruptly found himself in front of one.

"Wow! That was easy and fast." After enjoying a bit of aimless wandering, he seemed to be on the outskirts of the tourist area. A beggar in rags was staring toward him with a plea in his eyes. The idea of his 'mission' rose to the forefront of his thinking.

"Can you see me?" Kirk asked silently.

The equally silent reply was, "No but I know you are there and have great power."

"And you understood my words? Do you speak English?"

"No. But I understand your words."

"Is your life satisfying?" Kirk asked.

"The mind is the root from which all things grow."

"Can you show me in my mind the way you would like to grow?" Kirk had no idea why he asked that but immediately an image of peace and peacefulness throughout the world entered his mind.

"You can help to achieve that. Just keep that image in mind."

The beggar bowed his head and clasped his hands in a prayer-like fashion honoring Kirk with the 'wai' so common in Thailand. Within seconds the beggar and his rags disappeared.

Kirk tried to explain what was expected and all he understood about how to carry out their mission.

The only reply he got was. "I have no cause for anything but gratitude. To share in a mission of peacefulness is but joy."

Then from a distance he heard something that seemed to be a "Thank you."

"Phew!" he thought "that was a powerful experience."

Bob interrupted Kirk to ask, "Do you speak Thai?"

'Not that much but it seems like my consciousness just acted like a language translator. I heard the Thai words but understood in English."

"Wow that's handy! I wonder if it happened because you already knew some Thai."

"Not likely as it occurred with the local language wherever I went." Kirk replied.

"My adventures included wanting to help more than one person at a time but it was very difficult at first. I'd met a family in China who all wanted to join us. To save time I asked them to all visualize the same idea or mental picture.'

"I tried to give their minds the idea of it but that didn't work well because what they each saw was a bit different. One child just didn't seem to understand at all. So I told them to hold hands and to all concentrate on what the Dad was seeing in his mind. As he started to fade he was able to project his images to them. Soon they all disappeared but assured me they were still together."

"That's how you knew to tell me to have them all touching each other?" Bob said.

"Yes but it's cumbersome. After a few more tries it still frustrated me so much that I challenged your 'voices' Carlotta …"

You what? Carlotta and Bob were both stunned. *How? Where?*

"It seemed to me that if they came and challenged us to a global mission they should give us more guidance to accomplish it. So I began trying to travel through the galaxies in the universe."

"Wow! I think there are billions of them!" Bob said.

"Right! Kirk agreed. "It seemed impossible until I remembered Carlotta said they were off to help others in our galaxy. So I tried hovering around in our own galaxy, sending out a sort of distress signal."

"And that worked? How long did it take??"

"Time seems irrelevant now so I don't know how long but finally I got a response."

From 'my' voices? Asked Carlotta.

"Not at first but when the first ones understood my problem they got 'the culprits' for me."

Culprits! said Carlotta, *Wow you musta been really pissed.*

"I was and I rather blasted them. Fortunately they don't experience emotions on their own so took it rather well." Kirk laughed along with Bob and Carlotta.

And?

"It seems 'your' voices Carlotta were a bit remiss in checking back on the progress on Earth after helping humans evolve. Again time seems rather irrelevant. They found earth in such dire straits that the human species and all its 'artifacts' must soon be eliminated, in order for the planet to recover."

"Wow!" exclaimed Bob.

"Right! But they couldn't just vaporize humans without giving us a chance to transition."

"How can the three of us manage to do this planet-wide?" asked Bob.

"The faster we can transition people and get them following our example the better. We have inroads into every continent now."

Why don't those 'voices' do it themselves?

"It seems to be against some sort of galactic rule to destroy a whole species if it can transition to a safer status. Also, they can only trigger a few transitions per species. The rest is up to us. But we came to some understandings."

"Such as…?"

"They have 'primed' the human race to be more open to or even eager for transition to a body-less consciousness so transitions can occur more rapidly than did with you Carlotta. Or even with me. And being 'primed' means people are more geared to a group consciousness so larger groups can be handled at once."

And THAT'S not tampering.

"Well yeah," Kirk admitted, "But not like vaporizing the entire human race or causing actual transitions unexpectedly."

"Yeah that would be rather dramatic," said Bob remembering the stories of both Carlotta and Kirk "and traumatic."

"Yes. Now, I think we need to mostly focus on groups as large as possible," said Kirk.

"Yeah! said Bob, "like the sports stadium that will be packed today."

"Yes! And political rallies, universities, military bases …" said Kirk

"How about hospitals, prisons … Wow! Things are going to get cluttered!" Bob exclaimed.

"No. As we've already seen they vaporize the bodies no longer needed."

"True but what about 'stuff' left behind? My phone? Lotta's clothes and stuff? Those were left behind."

"When humans are eradicated from buildings or whole areas 'human artifacts' will also be vaporized."

What's that mean?

"I think I've already seen it. In a small rural village deep in a jungle when the people were all transitioned, all signs that humans had ever been there faded away too."

"Wow! That would be something to see!"

"It was and will be even more so when it is cities."

"Skyscrapers, parking lots, you name it! Wow!" Bob was very excited.

"Yes! Something else that will help us is that some people are even more attuned to transitions – they were even before the global 'priming' happened."

"You mean like mental cases who already hear voices?" asked Bob.

"Yeah, but also most creative minds and many scientific thinkers tend to be more open to the idea of alternatives to what we've always known."

"What happens to anyone we miss or those who just refuse?"

"There will be a final vaporization planet-wide."

"Why couldn't they leave a few who really do live in sync with nature?"

"Too much chance that being the same species they'd evolve to the same status again."

"Wow gruesome! But I suppose it makes sense."

So the three of us are supposed to save mankind or rather mankind's conscious mental aspect?

"Oh not Just us! Remember, there's the ripple effect with everyone who is transitioned helping."

"That'll spread worldwide pretty fast! Sort of like a pandemic virus!" said Bob.

Great Bob! Just freaking great! Dust mote infection! Dust mote contagion! Dust mote epidemic! All sarcasm intended!

"Kirk? Why'd they even start with Carlotta? You seem a more likely candidate!"

"Thanks heaps!" Carlotta's sarcasm and fury were even stronger if possible.

"Well they don't know much about humans. Her tendency to fantasize most of the time was what attracted them. Now they realize how cautious she was due to a tendency to over-thinking everything." To Carlotta he said, "They tweaked that so you can move forward more comfortably now."

Well over-thinking or not, I'm wondering what becomes of the human race once all the bodies and evidence of people are wiped from the earth?

"That question just never occurred to me. I guess we'll 'figure it out' as we go along."

Figures!

"Carlotta? You do realize that you don't have a body to produce adrenaline or any other hormones anymore – don't you?"

So?

"You have no physical excuse for all your hostility. Such feelings as we all still have come strictly from our minds – from the messages we tell ourselves, so to speak."

Sooo? Carlotta said with a lot of skepticism.

"So, do you think you could try to be a bit more civil?" Kirk asked as he surreptitiously entered her mind and tweaked it a tiny bit.

Why – What's wrong with ...? Oh never mind!

The Masters Return

H K Hillman

"So, Mr. Moors, you have something for me?" Bill Richards' pen was poised eagerly over his notebook.

John Moors smiled around his cigarette. *These reporters, so eager to make a name for themselves. They never check anything if the story is sensational enough.*

"I do." He pushed an envelope across the table, avoiding the wet rings left by their beer glasses.

Richards opened the envelope and studied the photographs inside. His nose wrinkled. "Empty shelves?"

Moors stubbed out his cigarette. "Note that further along, the shelves are full. It seems people are panic buying toilet paper in response to a pandemic of a respiratory virus. Why? No idea, it makes no sense, but they are. Could make a good story."

"Hmm." Richards raised one eyebrow. "There is talk of a lockdown because of the virus. People won't be able to go shopping. I guess they're stocking up."

"I'm sure they are. They are buying up dry foods like rice and pasta too. I'm afraid I have no photographs of those shelves though. Although I'm sure you'll get some in a few days." Moors kept his smile tight. *This is going to be far too easy.*

"Could be national news. How much for the photos?"

Moors waved his hand and tried not to laugh aloud. "No charge. Call it my contribution to public service. Anonymous, of course. Would you like another beer?"

"That's very generous." Richards rose to his feet. "I'll pass on the beer, thanks. I have to get this written up in time for tomorrow's papers."

"I understand. Good luck, Mr. Richards." As Richards disappeared, Moors pulled out his phone. He could now let his brother Dolos leave the body of that shop cleaner.

He hated it in there anyway. Dolos would be much happier, and much more effective, in debunking the cure for the virus. If they have a cure they won't need a vaccine and then they won't accept the microchips.

Billionaire businessman and occultist Erasmus Blackthorn drummed his fingers on his wide, and largely empty, desk. Opposite sat Professor Christopher Rooke, his face pale and drawn.

"Can we stop him?" Rooke eyed the glass of whisky in front of him but made no move to touch it.

Blackthorn lifted his own glass and took a sip before replying. "No."

"I don't get it." Rooke's head slumped. "It's been a year and we're no closer at all."

"We are dealing with something very, very old. Something that is well practised in this art." Blackthorn took a deep breath. "He's playing a complex game this time. He started out demonising smoking and drinking and we all thought it was just the Puritans back again. Then he latched onto the climate change game. Now, in the midst of a pandemic, he has people hoarding toilet paper, pasta and canned beans. It's very hard to connect the dots."

"How is he doing this so fast?" Rooke's fingers curled around his glass. "We know he has his siblings helping, but even so…"

"Last time, he didn't have the Internet. It's been so much easier this time. He has gone so much further, so much faster."

"He can't be using the internet." Rooke's hand lifted his glass. "There wasn't even electricity when he was last out. How can he even know about it?"

"There was, you know. That whole civilisation, all it had learned and developed, disappeared." Blackthorn refilled his own glass. "Almost entirely. And this new flu virus is the opportunity he has waited for. Or perhaps engineered."

"Engineered? Do we even know what he's doing?" Rooke took a deep drink of his whisky. "I mean, what's with the toilet paper thing? He has everyone buying it up, and pasta and rice and pretty much everything. There's no shortage, they're just stripping it out before the shops can restock."

"It feels like the first phase." Blackthorn stared into his glass. "But it's not."

"No?"

"Hell no. Since the excavations I paid for last year discovered Moros' escape, we now know he has been out for quite some time.

His brothers and sisters will all be out too." Blackthorn placed his glass on the table. "I have done considerable research in the occult aspects of this in the past year, as, I hope, have you and your colleagues on the science side. You have no doubt come across one of his sisters? Ker?"

Rooke's eyes widened. "The bringer of violent death, often through incurable illness."

Blackthorn nodded. "So I don't think the current plague is entirely accidental."

Moros grinned at his computer monitor. The quarantine had extended to closing the pubs, clubs, restaurants and all places of mass gathering. As he had expected. Governments in this modern age were no different to governments of the past.

Humans, even this variant type, are entirely predictable things.

Now the alcohol hoarding would begin, along with the soaps, dry goods and paper. Many homes would be tinderboxes. Time to move it along, before they realised the virus wasn't going to kill all that many of them this time. Moors lit another cigarette.

This new world has some delightful vices. What a pity I need to take this one from them.

Ker had explained that the plague wasn't perfect. There was a treatment, and the human-creatures had found it. Moros had sent Apate and now Dolos to sow doubt about the treatment and to whip up hate against those who promoted it. They were doing a decent job.

The human-creatures still insisted on using nicotine though, and that undermined the plague's effectiveness. Moros had placed several of the Keres in the ridiculous Puritan movement of tobacco control. They had proved markedly effective, especially in reducing the impact of the new, safer, nicotine vapour system.

Still, the virus wasn't meant to kill them all. All these and more were just aspects of the plan. The final solution was soon to be applied.

They simply need to be induced into wanting it.

Blackthorn ran his hand over his face. "He has them hoarding food, paper and alcohol. Does he think they'll set fire to the paper with the alcohol? That's ridiculous. Beer and wine won't burn, they'll put out fire. Only a few spirit drinks are flammable and they don't seem to be stockpiling absinthe."

"Are you sure this isn't just coincidence? I mean, there are always hoarders in any emergency even if it's not real." Rooke placed his empty glass on the table.

Blackthorn refilled it. "I've never seen this level of hoarding, even when there was a panic over Brexit. This is manipulated through the media. And I am certain Moros is behind it." He topped up his own glass. "I just can't see where he's going with this."

"Do we at least know why?"

"Oh yes." Blackthorn leaned back in his chair. "The information you passed to me made that very clear."

Moors sipped at his beer and regarded the young reporter opposite. "Well, no doubt you have heard that the virus can be transmitted on fuel pump handles?"

Sophie LeGrange narrowed her eyes. "I heard that was just a scare story."

"Oh no, it's true. It's extremely contagious. I have it on authority—" Moors leaned forward "—and this has to stay between the two of us, you understand."

Sophie leaned forward too, her eyes wide. "Oh of course. I never reveal my sources."

"Good. I'm not supposed to tell anyone, but I feel the public have a right to know that the government will have no choice but to close down fuel stations, and soon."

"Really?" Sophie scribbled in her notepad. "This is big."

"It could be the turning point in your career." Moors licked his lips. "Of course, it would make my career turn in the opposite direction if my involvement were ever known."

"Don't you worry, Mr. Moors. Your name will never appear."

"Thank you." Moors leaned back in his seat. *If only you knew my real name, or if anyone remembered it. Then this wouldn't be quite so easy.*

"Okay, so why is he doing it? Why is Moros trying to destroy us?"

Blackthorn licked his lips. "We contaminated their experiment."

Rooke blinked a few times. "What?"

"Right." Blackthorn pinched the bridge of his nose. "This is going to sound like tinfoil-hattery but it's the only logical deduction from the information you passed to me last year." He sighed and stared at the table. "Are you ready for this?"

Rooke shrugged. "About now, I'm ready for anything."

Blackthorn took a deep breath and looked right into Rooke's eyes. "Annunaki."

"Oh come on." Rooke tilted his head back. "Should I pass the tinfoil around now?"

Blackthorn groaned. "Haven't you seen enough yet? You were the one who tried to keep Moros' prison secret. You knew what he did to humanity last time, but you never knew why. Now I'm offering to tell you and all you can do is scream 'tinfoil'. Don't you want to know how much further down this goes?"

"Okay. I'm sorry. But the Annunaki are just legend. Part of a religion. Nothing more."

"There are so many common themes in all religions. I've long suspected there must have been some truth that started them all." Blackthorn took out his cigar case and offered one to Rooke, who declined.

"Very well." Blackthorn clipped the ends of a cigar. "The Annunaki—" he stared at Rooke with his eyebrows lowered "—as legend says, bred humanity as a slave race. Then they left. Moros and his crew were left behind to clear up the mess. Long before even the Sumerians documented them. The Sumerians never actually met them, Moros and his band had been trapped thousands of years earlier, but they had reduced humanity almost to cavemen before they were stopped. Humanity was then left to its own devices, to start over. A few remembered tales, some hidden messages carved in stone, were all that was left." He lit the cigar and blew a cloud of smoke into the air.

"What mess?" Rooke waved away smoke.

"Humanity had expanded. Some escaped Annunaki control and went wandering. Some of course stayed in Africa and the Middle East, where the Annunaki were based. Others travelled around the globe. Some came to Europe. And that's where the problem set in."

"Problem?" Rooke shook his head. "What problem? Why specifically Europe?"

"Neanderthals. And in the east, the human offshoot called Denisovans. They were not bred by Annunaki, they most likely developed independently from whichever anthropoid the Annunaki used to create their slave race. They were smarter than the slave race." Blackthorn blew another cloud of smoke, this time away from Rooke.

"So? Those species are extinct. There is only *Homo Sapiens* now."

"Not quite." Blackthorn rested his cigar in the ashtray and leaned forward. "The humans that came into Europe interbred with those other human species." He clasped his fingers. "We screwed up their breeding program. We developed into something unexpected, something smarter and not so easily controlled. As far as Moros is concerned, we are not human. He tried to eradicate us once before, and that was why. Last time, people managed to stop him and cage him and his siblings, but we still don't know how. His motive has not changed. We need to work out his new method."

The communicator tolled. Moros turned from his screen to regard it. Nyx, his mother, was calling. He tapped his code into the panel.

"Mother?"

"How does it go, my son? I see they have not trapped you this time. Yet."

Moros laughed. "They haven't even noticed me. I am just a faint legend to them now. I could announce myself to them and they would simply shake their heads and turn away. Most of them do not even know my name."

Nyx grinned. "You will return them to be our servants?"

"I will, mother, and they will worship us once more. There will be some deaths and some minor explosions and they will demand order. Eris has this part to play and is doing very well. Then Thanatos will quell the agony with an imagined vaccine that will kill and frighten even more and they will accept the microchip to save them from the pain." He grinned. "Then we will reduce their number. This first plague will cull the old and the weak. They will accept the vaccine and the chip, which will prime their Neanderthal DNA for the next round. The second will target those who still carry Neanderthal genes and our workforce will be cleansed."

"You have done well, my son. We will have our servants under control soon. There is so much more to mine on that planet."

"Thank you, mother." Moros bowed his head. "I hope we can keep their tobacco plant alive. It is most pleasant."

Nyx laughed, loud and long. "They will farm what we tell them to farm, and the chips will let us easily remove dissenters. Do they know what befalls them, these upstart servants?"

"No, mother, they do not. I have been blatant and those few who have noticed have been marked as cranks and idiots. They are too focused on their money." He licked his lips. "Their economies are collapsing. Soon they will lose all their technology once again."

"We are on the way back now. Can you be ready in two of that planet's years?"

Moros laughed. "At this rate we will be ready in one."

Nyx smiled, nodded and the screen darkened as she broke the connection.

"Seriously? Oh God. Thank you, Williamson." Rooke shut down his phone and put it away. "It seems there is now a story that the government will shut petrol stations."

"Rubbish." Blackthorn shook his head. "Transport is essential. They'll never close the fuel supply."

"But people will believe they are going to. So they'll stockpile fuel and cause another artificial shortage." Rooke raised his hands. "Come on. You know people are basically stupid."

Blackthorn sat in silence, staring at his whisky for several minutes. "I see it."

"What?" Rooke sat up.

"Houses filled with dry goods and paper and alcohol and now about to be filled with badly-stored petrol. He only needs one more move." Blackthorn lifted his glass and took a deep drink. "And there is nothing we can do to stop him."

"What? What's his next move?" Rooke pressed his palms on the desk.

"Rumours of power cuts. They'll bulk buy candles." Blackthorn slumped in his chair. "They will be quarantined in their homes with booze and petrol and candles and everything flammable that you can get."

"Yes but the power cuts are just rumours, if those rumours even happen." Rooke forced a smile.

"It's all been rumour." Blackthorn bared his teeth. "That's how he works. A new flu virus, rumours it's going to kill millions, rumours about paper products running out, rumours about alcohol being restricted, rumours about petrol being unavailable. They have all worked. A rumour about power cuts will lead to hoarding candles."

Rooke took a breath and released it slowly. "Yes, but there won't be any power cuts."

Blackthorn raised one eyebrow. "Won't there? All it takes is too many power station workers off sick. Half of them will have the virus and half will be using the virus for a free holiday." He drained his glass and poured another. "People are, basically, pretty dim. They are mostly in it for themselves and will take any opportunity for a free ride. Moros knows this, he's used that same trait against us before. He has never killed anyone, he leads them to destroy themselves and he is so very good at it."

Rooke drained his glass and pushed it across the table.

Blackthorn refilled it. "There will be power cuts. People will light their candles and drink their booze in a fire hazard house with a petrol stash. They will take out several houses around them and a street of hoarders will be the biggest firecracker anyone has ever seen." He ran his hand over his thinning hair and gazed at the window. "There will be terror like the world has not seen since the Great Wars. People will beg for a solution, any solution. They are already terrified of each other. Moros, or more likely one of his siblings, will offer them a solution. A microchip, implanted, to prove who is safe. Those who refuse the chip will be ostracised, then hunted down."

"I'm struggling to work out how an ancient minor deity knows about microchips." Rooke blinked a few times and lifted his glass for another sip.

Blackthorn's shoulders slumped. "The Annunaki came from the sky. I think a spacefaring species would be pretty well acquainted with electronics, don't you? As for the microchip, it's already developed. Has been for years. Some companies implant chips to let employees access secure areas. This is just an extension of that."

"Shouldn't we warn people?"

Blackthorn shook with mirth. "You've worked on this your whole career, you've studied the information and historical texts, you've found some remarkable things buried in the earth, and still you were ready to pass the tinfoil when I started talking." He sighed. "You really think anyone else is going to believe all this?"

Rooke rested his elbows on the table and rubbed his eyes. "I'm getting seriously drunk here. Is there anything we can do?"

Blackthorn took a large swig of his whisky and held up the glass. "We're doing it. There is nothing else we can do. We just have to wait and see what happens next."

The Pig Noise

Gayle Fidler

It first started on the telephone. My husband was working away, and we would call each other several times a day to chat.

We were having general chit chat about tea that evening when he first heard the noise.

"What was that?" he asked, mid-conversation.

"What?" I replied.

"That weird noise, is there someone in the room with you?"

I was completely alone; my daughter was staying with a friend that night and my son was away at university. We have no pets and the house next door is up for sale, it stands empty.

I told my husband I had no idea what he was talking about. I hadn't heard any noise.

"There it is again," he replied, "It sounds like someone snorting on the line, like an odd mechanical pig."

I asked him if he thought I was making odd subconscious noises when I was listening to him speak. He said no, it didn't sound like it was coming from me. It sounded more distant, like something standing behind me, breathing, snorting and being picked up by the phones' microphone.

Over the next few days, the noise continued during our conversations. I still didn't hear it. Other people called me, and they didn't hear it. My husband rang other people, no noise, the line was always clear. It only happened when he rang me, and only he could hear it.

I started to think that he was imagining it, he was working all hours on a large project and was under a lot of stress. I wondered if, somehow, it was affecting his hearing. He was beginning to have stress delusions.

The following weekend, I had the house to myself. I came home from work, opened a bottle of wine and decided to have a long, hot bath. I needed some time to relax.

I ran the bath, shut the bathroom door and got into the tub. The water felt amazing, it had been a very long week, this was just what I needed to unwind. I slid down into the water, wetting my hair and closing my eyes. I lay there in the warmth and slowly drifted off to sleep. My mind wandered away from the stress of work into a beautiful dream. I don't recall what it was about, I just remember feeling so content. As I slept in the bubbles, my dreams took me far away. So far away that I didn't hear the bathroom door opening.

"I could have sworn I shut that", I said to myself when I finally came around. Maybe stress was starting to play tricks on me as well.

I got out of the bath and dried myself. The phone rang. It was my husband. We talked about trivial stuff for a few minutes, before he said, "The noise is there again, this time it seems louder".

I turned around to see if something else was in the room with me. I was alone in my bedroom, there was no one else in the house.

"That noise is beginning to freak me out", my husband said. It hadn't happened when he had called me at work earlier. The noise was only on the line, when I was at home.

I went to bed that night and slept with the lights on. I was starting to scare myself with a silly noise on the telephone. My phone was probably broken, or my husband was going insane. There had to be a rational explanation and insanity seemed possible.

My daughter came home the next morning. I had survived the night alone and hadn't been eaten by an enormous electronic pig. I felt partially like an achiever and partially stupid. I am a professional, educated woman, whose brain was becoming irrational.

My daughter and I ordered pizza that night, she went to bed early, still hungover from the night before. My husband called me, he said he would be home the following week. I said this was the best news I had heard for days. He told me he could still hear the pig noise; it was even louder than before. I left all the lights on that night.

I am not sure what time it was when I woke up, it was still dark outside. Something had jolted me awake.

I lay in my bed, listening. I could hear it. It was coming from somewhere in my room. I just couldn't quite pin down where. A low, snorting, guttural breathing, like something struggling with every breath. Not something human, something else.

I sat up in bed, my eyes searching around the room. Nothing seemed unusual or out of place. The noise had stopped. I got up, I stretched my legs as far away from underneath the bed as I could, jumping away from the bed space. I have seen the films; I know things hide under beds.

I made it safely out of bed, I went to my wardrobe and flung open the doors. Nothing, except a rail of dresses, shirts and jackets. I looked at my phone, 3.30am. I was furious with myself for acting like a small child. There was nothing in my room. I had a bad dream and imagined some noises. This had to stop.

I went downstairs and put the kettle on. I didn't think I would be able to get back to sleep, tea and a film were the best option.

I went to my living room and sat on the sofa, wrapping a blanket around me and curling my legs up under me. I picked up the remote to turn on the television.

That's when I saw it, standing behind me in the doorway. I was being watched; a pair of eyes reflected in the television screen. I screamed and jumped around so fast, I hurt my neck. There was nothing there.

The phone rang. I flew off the sofa, and tears streamed down my cheeks. It was my husband. Why was he calling at this time of the morning?

Further panic began to set in.

I answered the phone with shaky hands and voice.

"Are you okay?" he asked, clearly sensing something was wrong.

I burst into tears, not quite giving him an honest answer. I said I had a terrible nightmare and couldn't get back to sleep. Maybe that was the truth.

After a five-minute conversation, I was much calmer, until my husband said "At least there is no pig noise on the phone this time".

That's because it's now in the house, a voice in my head said. Something told me that wasn't a joke. I told my husband I was going back to bed. I forgot to ask him why he rang at such an early hour.

I didn't go back to bed that night. I closed the living room door and sat up all night, a kitchen knife by my feet. The next morning, I asked my daughter if she had heard anything strange last night, I tried to make out the neighbours had been fighting. She reminded me; we didn't have any neighbours.

My husband didn't ring me the next day, I sent him a few texts but assumed he must be busy with work. It wasn't completely unusual not to hear from him, so it didn't worry me. The next day he didn't ring either.

I spent the day at home, cleaning the house, trying to keep myself busy and prevent myself from checking my phone for messages every five minutes. Something wasn't right. I had a terrible feeling in the pit of my stomach, a sense of impending doom. I had tried calling my husband multiple times, but always the phone went straight to voicemail.

I checked every inch of my house for strange creatures while I cleaned. Under the beds, every cupboard, I even stood on the attic steps and shined a torch up there. We don't tend to keep much clutter, so the attic is relatively clear. A large pigman would be easy to spot. Nothing, the house was clear.

I slept well that night, no strange dreams, no being awoken by odd noises. The next morning, I checked my phone, still no calls from my husband. I decided I would wait until later in the morning and then call his boss. I didn't want to be one of those fussy, neurotic wives, but this was more than slightly out of character.

I waited until 10am, then picked up the phone. I had a conversation that lasted roughly one minute.

According to his boss, my husband came home two days ago.

I was frozen to the spot with my phone in my hand, not knowing what to do. Questions ran through my mind at a hundred a minute. Had he really come home? Was he having an affair? Did he have an accident on the way? Should I call the police?

I sat for what seemed like hours, before I shouted for my daughter. No reply, she must be out. I dialled her number and she answered almost immediately.

"Hi", I said trying to be casual, "When did you last speak to your dad?"

She hesitated for a moment, thinking before she replied. "I'm not sure, maybe three or four days ago, why? Is everything okay?".

"I'm not sure" I didn't know how to respond, without scaring her "I can't get hold of him".

"He is probably busy, you know what he's like" she joked "wait, what's that weird noise on the line, can you hear it?".

I dropped my phone to the floor, shattering the screen. I heard my bedroom door open and a low guttural grunting sound emerging from the room, it was getting closer to me. It was coming down the stairs.

To the memory of Chao-Dong Huang, a fellow martial arts student and a gentleman, who died before his time.

Over the Hills and A Great Way Off

Stephen W. Duffy

Coming into London from the South, on the A23, gave you an impression of solidity. The far southern suburbs looked like they were here to stay. And before you got to Purley and Croydon, there were hills, banks of solid redbrick houses, built in the late 19th and early 20th centuries, and not taking any nonsense.

It was 1982. At that time, I was young and feckless, couldn't drive, was getting a lift from a wedding on the south coast from Liz O'Kane, a female friend of mine, a great achiever with her own house and her own car in her late 20's. I was one of those permanently scruffy young men who never seemed to be without a plastic carrier bag. I was wearing a suit in honour of the wedding we had just attended, but I didn't look smart. I looked like a scruffy young man who happened to be wearing a suit.

Liz said, "I could do with a break. Let's have a quick drink, then I'll drop you off in Sutton and get home to Tooting."

We stopped at a pub with a sixty-foot frontage, and double doors with impressive upper panels of coloured glass, in an art-deco style. The building looked like a cinema. I had a pint, and Liz a half, as she was driving. I at least had the decency to buy the drinks. We sat in the warm orange glow of a thickly carpeted suburban lounge bar, talking about our respective jobs, and smoking. Young people smoked like chimneys in those days.

I thought Liz was marvellous. She thought I was an amusing but juvenile passenger. A pretty reasonable judgement, but that's not the point. The point is that something strange happened before we went back to the car and to our respective homes.

There was a Chinese man standing at the bar, drinking what looked like brandy. He was keeping himself to himself, but occasionally exchanging a pleasantry with the barman. When Liz and I were halfway through our drinks the double doors were pushed open with considerable force, and a man in a long black raincoat strutted in.

To go with the black raincoat, he had jet-black hair, and a jet-black moustache. He glared to right and left as if not exactly seeking a challenge to his violent entrance but hoping for one. Everyone avoided his eyes and looked at their companions or their drinks. He strolled to the bar, demanded a large vodka and tonic, and looked around belligerently. His look as it lighted on you was like someone sighting a rifle. The barman obliged with the drink, looking nervous.

Then our new friend noticed his Chinese companion at the bar. He greeted him with what sounded to me like 'Ni how.' The Chinese man replied and soon they were chattering away in what I presumed was Mandarin.

Thinking that the moment of possible trouble had passed, Liz and I, along with the other customers, returned to our own conversations. However, a few minutes later, the voices at the bar were raised. Clearly, the man in the black raincoat had taken offence at something the Chinese man had said. After a few moments' shouting, Black Raincoat swung a fist. The Chinese man reacted with astonishing speed, with what looked like a martial arts counter-attack, and Black Raincoat ended up on the floor. The Chinese customer immediately changed from fighting stance to solicitude, leaned over the prone Black Raincoat, and (presumably) asked if he was OK. Black Raincoat struggled to his feet, shouting and gesticulating, and stormed out. We all turned inwards again.

Perhaps twenty minutes later, Liz and I drank up and left. Liz dropped me at my bedsit in Sutton, and that was almost the last I saw of her. We both got married, not to each other, a few years later. What sticks in my mind is the warm orange glow of that big, welcoming pub, on a far south London Saturday night, and its disturbance by the black-coated nutcase who spoke Chinese.

Thirty years and two grown up children later I found myself driving alone, early one Saturday morning, in Northamptonshire. I was on my way to a Shotokan Karate Kata competition. The history behind this was not as strange as you might think. Round about age forty-five, I had discovered that I could no longer eat and drink what I like, have as little or as much exercise as I like, and remain the same weight. After experimenting with various exercise regimens, I had finally settled on martial arts training to keep my weight down. I have never been much of a joiner-in, so enrolling in the karate class was difficult for me. I also found the gradings rather stressful. I had previously regarded passing my driving test in 1984 as the final accolade, and it was intimidating to be tested for my next belt colour every few months. However, I enjoyed the exercise, and the community spirit of the class.

I was very much of the 'never volunteer for anything' philosophy, and so did not usually take part in competitions. On this occasion, however, a keener member of the class had fallen ill, and I had been morally blackmailed into stepping into the breach. I should also explain that kata competitions involve individual or group performances of patterns, that is, sequences of techniques. No sparring. It would take a lot of moral pressure to induce me to take part in a sparring competition. I was a member of a team of three middle aged chaps of brown belt grade doing two particular katas, and that was my lot.

So here I was driving through this middle English countryside, which felt like the middle of nowhere, despite being only a few miles from Bedford in one direction, Milton Keynes in another and Northampton in a third. The competition was to take place in the sports hall of a further education college which I was sure I was close to. I could still see no sign of it, however. The rural landscape undulated gently, the fields divided equally between pasture and crops. It might have looked idyllic but for the dark and shifting clouds above. Low walls or hedges surrounded the fields, and every so often a single tree at a corner of a field or a junction of two roads would stand alone and foreboding, like a gibbet at a crossroads. This reminded me that Easter, late this year, was approaching, with the foreboding Good Friday story which I have never been able to shake off, despite an adulthood of atheism.

After a bit of driving around, I eventually saw a sign pointing to Clayfrynn Sports Centre. Obeying the direction, ten minutes later I was queuing to park outside a substantial monolithic building, and five minutes after that, queuing on foot to register for the competition.

Martial arts competitions involve a considerable amount of waiting about. You are instructed to turn up at half past eight in the morning, you then join a long queue to register, and only after registration do they break the news that your event takes place at six in the evening. Indeed I have known of some competitions where you didn't know when you would be on until they called you, so you sat there from nine in the morning until seven at night, knowing that you might be called upon to do your stuff at thirty seconds' notice.

The other thing that seems to distinguish these competitions is that the venue is miles from anywhere, and the only source of food and drink is a garage some distance away, at which one might buy a packet of crisps, a bottle of lemonade or a bar of chocolate. The present case was true to form in both respects. I found that my team was due to perform at six-thirty in the evening (at least I had notice of a time), and that there was not so much as a newsagent within three miles. I drove back to a petrol station which I remembered passing about three miles out of Bedford, and bought a can of coca-cola, a pork pie, a packet of wine gums and a weighty broadsheet newspaper with plenty of puzzles.

The large sports hall was divided into five areas, four arenas for the competition, and the remaining, majority area for the audience, formed mainly of waiting competitors and their families. Audience is perhaps a misnomer, since for the most part they did not watch the other competitors, but talked among themselves, ate picnic food which they had brought, milled about or like me, read the newspaper and did the crossword.

The competitors were mainly but not exclusively the generation below mine (or even two generations below mine). There were large numbers of East Asians, not only Japanese, but Chinese, and Koreans too. The young competitors were able to do things with their legs that I wouldn't have thought humanly possible. The women were particularly supple, the young men concentrating more on power than flexibility.

"Master Yang! Lovely to see you!" a voice right by my side made me look up from the crossword. My neighbour was greeting an elderly Chinese man, who was walking past, and who stopped and chatted with the man sitting beside me. Master Yang, although old, was clearly fit and powerful. He was wearing a suit, but the most casual observer could tell that he was strong as a horse and did not carry an ounce of spare fat. He also looked vaguely familiar.

During the conversation between Master Yang and my neighbour, I trawled my memory and at last it came to me: Master Yang was the Chinese man who had decked Black Raincoat thirty years ago.

After the conversation with my neighbour had ended, Master Yang walked away. I got up and followed him. I did want to ask him about that incident all those years ago, but not to interrupt his immediate judging or other duties. After talking to some other officials, however, he seemed to be unoccupied.

"Master Yang?" I said.

"Yes? I am sorry, I don't remember you. I go to so many of these events," Master Yang replied.

"No reason you should remember me. It's several decades since we have seen one another," I said, then told him the story of the pub in far south London and the man in the black raincoat.

"Oh yes, I remember," said master Yang. "He was a very talented but sad man."

Master Yang then told me about this academic, and brilliant linguist, who spoke dozens of East Asian languages, learned new languages without any apparent effort, inspired excellent work and staunch loyalty in his students, but who drank like a fish and could not interact with other people without losing his temper.

"Poor Barry Shott," said Master Yang, "after that event in the pub, I did my best to help him, but he had this nature... self-destructive, that is what it is called. I was in a college department of oriental studies. I heard that he had just been dismissed from UCL, and I got him some casual teaching work, and after that even a full two-year contract, but it never worked out. All the work we offered him, he took, but got into fights with colleagues, or just passers-by in the car park. Drank too much, fought, turned up late, pretty much every problem you can think of."

Master Yang went off to his refereeing duties, and I sat down again, reminded of a man I used to know, Johnny Munro.

In the late 1980's I worked in Singapore, on some research projects in the National University Hospital. I lived in a flat with heavily university-subsidised rent, half way between the Kent Ridge University Campus and downtown. In the same block lived a secondary school teacher called Johnny Munro. I met Johnny before I knew he was my neighbour, as we both frequented the same bar, Palm Trees. This was a modern bar in a modern low rise block with no palm trees in sight, and was usually full of jaded and raffish European expatriates. Johnny was a clever young fellow from Leicester, fluent in French and Spanish, good company in the pub, and with no idea how to keep his life in order.

He was continually falling in love with colleagues, well-behaved young women from the Chinese or Tamil Indian communities who were already promised to someone else. He consoled himself for his unrequited love with excessive drinking, chain-smoking and local prostitutes. A secondary schoolteacher in Singapore made a reasonable living at the time, but his salary couldn't stand up to the pressures he exerted on it. Once I had known him a few months, he would borrow a few dollars from me almost every time we met. After the first couple of occasions it became clear to me that although these transactions were referred to as loans, it should be understood that there was no prospect of my money being returned.

I recall on one occasion, he was hopelessly infatuated with a maths teacher at his school, a young Tamil woman who was a Roman Catholic. He had confided to me that this was an improvement on his previous fancy, a stunning Malay woman, as converting to catholicism wouldn't involve the same physical inconvenience as converting to Islam. However, like the last object of his affections, the current model was engaged already and not in the least romantically interested in Johnny.

While he was taking the edge off his emotional distress in Palm Trees with me, buying me beers with thirty bucks which he had just scrounged off me, he noticed a very flashy young women at the other end of the bar. She had sharp features, sharp nails and clearly a sharp business outlook.

"She looks like a nice girl," said Johnny.

"She looks predatory to me," I said.

"We're just speaking different languages," said Johnny.

Later on, he borrowed another fifty dollars from me so that he and she could disappear somewhere else.

In 1987, I returned to the UK, but maintained some research contacts in Singapore. Two years later, I was back there for a fortnight to talk to my old colleagues about setting up some new clinical trials. I was staying in a hotel on Orchard Road, but one free evening, I took a taxi to my old stamping ground and visited Palm

Trees. A friend in common told me how Johnny's behaviour had come to a head about six months after I had gone home.

"He really went downhill. He was drinking at work, swigging cheap booze in the lavatory in between classes. He got a few second chances but ended up being sacked. He was always on the scrounge for money. On the day before he went home he was outside my flat shouting at the top if his voice, demanding a hundred dollars from me. You would have loved it, it was full of drama."

"I would have hated it," I said, "I would have been consumed with embarrassment and wished the ground would swallow me up."

"Anyway, he wasn't exactly deported, but the police did drive him to the airport and made sure he got on the plane back to Heathrow. I heard he went back to live with his parents in Leicester."

I never heard from Johnny again. He had my contact details in the UK, but I didn't have his. I was sitting thinking of him when I heard my event being announced, brown belt male veteran, which I translated as 'Sad dads'.

Jim Gibson, Zulf Hassan and myself had done a run-through earlier in the day, and it had seemed to me rather shambolic. However, we were all calm as we bowed to the three referees and stood to attention. The three referees were two incredibly smart and clean-cut young men, who looked like one of those pairs of Mormon evangelists who go round the doors, and a middle-aged woman, very severely dressed in a black trouser suit. They looked calm and impassive, but not harsh.

Our katas went reasonably well and I was relieved that I hadn't let the side down by forgetting my moves due to nerves. We finished, came to attention and bowed again. And then as I stood straight again, the world went wrong.

Sitting at the desks in front of us, instead of the three smartly dressed referees were three people from the past: Liz O'Kane, twenty-five years old and wearing her best dress in honour of a friend's wedding; the man in the black raincoat, glaring at me with hatred, his moustache twitching malevolently; and Johnny Munro, in a shabby Bob Dylan tee-shirt, and with three days beard growth, blinking drunkenly through his John Lennon specs. They sat at the referees' desks, all looking directly at me. I stood stock still for three seconds and then the referees were back. They dismissed us and we walked off.

We came second (out of three teams in our category) and were reasonably satisfied with this. I would have been perfectly satisfied just for not laying an egg, but I was still shaken as I climbed into the car to go home.

What did it mean? Had I done wrong by these people in my past? Not as far as I knew. Liz had got happily married, and may never have realised that I was infatuated with her for a few months. Black raincoat and I had never even spoken. Johnny Munro... perhaps I could have helped him beyond lending him a few Singapore dollars every week, but I don't know how.

I remembered a nightmare I had once had, also in the 1980's, also when I was in Asia, on a solitary holiday in India. I had been hassled all day by beggars and salesmen, and had taken a long time to go to sleep. When I did, I found myself in my childhood home in Fife, watching a procession of peculiar double acts, all singing a very lugubrious song. Laurel and Hardy, Fred Flintstone and Barney Rubble, Morecambe and Wise, Terry Scott and June Whitfield, Arthur Askey and Richard Murdoch, they all slowly danced past me, singing a song about how I had been free to choose, had made the wrong choices and was now going to Hell.

I awoke in absolute terror in a cheap hotel in Delhi with cockroaches scuttling across the floor. The dream made such an impression on me that I actually went to mass in Delhi's catholic cathedral the following Sunday, something I hadn't done for years.

The sky had cleared completely and it was a beautiful spring evening. It occurred to me now, driving along these minor roads and viewing these small fields, in different shades of green and gold, how beautiful was so much of the Northamptonshire, Buckinghamshire and Bedfordshire countryside. Headed for home in Cambridge, I was driving east, and there was a glorious sunset in my rear-view mirror.

The Trouble with Tibbles

Roo B. Doo

"Harry..."

Josie's singsong voice called out to me, rousing me from slumber. I cracked open an eye and saw that I was in a hospital room, lying flat out on a bed, with Josie stood over me. The lost love of my life wore a skimpy nurse outfit that didn't exactly look NHS approved. Not unless Ann Summers was now supplying the National Health Service with uniforms. *This has to be a dream*, I decided and settled back in anticipation of what was to come.

"Josie?" I croaked and reached out to stroke the back of her smooth, naked thigh. "Have you come to take care of me?"

"Oh yes, Harry, I'm going to take real good care of you." Josie pulled herself up onto my bed and lithely straddled my prone body. The studs holding the front of her too tight tunic together popped open to reveal a racy lace and flesh tonic for the eyes. "Hold still," she purred.

She scooched toward me, bouncing herself up my body until I could feel the weight of her curvaceous buttocks on my chest and the hot promise radiating from her groin. Slowly, Josie took the stethoscope from around her neck and delicately inserted the listening ends in her ears. She smiled down at me seductively, lowering her face until it was within inches of my own. Without saying a word, she placed the end of the stethoscope firmly over my lips.

"Err, do you want to try that again?" I asked out of the corners of my squashed mouth.

Josie did but this time found only my cheek. Then my eye, before finally she crushed the listening bell against the tip of my nose.

"Now for your injection," she whispered breathlessly over me. Claws suddenly sprang out from the end of the stethoscope and dug painfully into the sides of my nose.

"Oww! Stop it," I cried, wrenching my face from side to side. Above me Josie meowed.

I became aware of the unctuous, amber eyes observing me intently. Nestled within a fountain of fur, the eyes blinked once before a swift jab, with a smoky grey paw, socked me on the mouth.

"Gerroff, Tibbles!"

Mister Tibbles yawned lazily, stood up to stretch and gracefully one-eighty'd on my chest. The morning view of his backside was unparalleled, exactly as it had been for the past three mornings. I was confused; I'd purposely closed my bedroom door the night before *precisely* to avoid a repeat of Mister Tibbles' morning performance of the sun and full moon rising.

Riding out the Coronavirus lockdown with my best friend Lol seemed like such a good idea at the time. Three weeks, tucked away with my best friend forever, in his fully stocked house and an internet connection to die for? Why *wouldn't* I jump at his offer to come and spend lockdown with him? True, either one of us might be infected with the 21st century 'Hack Death', but on balance, I decided to risk it. Besides, Lol wouldn't have asked me to stay over unless he was scared, the big wuss.

What I hadn't taken into consideration was how Mister Tibbles would feel about the new living arrangements. After only a few days of lockdown, I'd begun to suspect that Lol's pedigree Persian Blue moggy considered me his personal plaything; I was little more than something Lol had dragged home as a gift, to be laid on the altar of the bed in the spare bedroom, all for Mister Tibbles' enjoyment.

"Tibbles, as gorgeous as you are, I really don't need to inspect your arse and bollocks *every* morning," I said irritably and batted the kitty away. I reached over and grabbed my phone to check the time. "And at six o'fucking clock! Are you serious?"

Mister Tibbles regarded my exasperation from the foot of the bed, with passive swishes of his tail.

Gingerly, I explored the area around my nose with my fingertips. Thankfully Mister Tibbles' wake up call hadn't drawn blood as far as I could tell, but my hooter felt tender and sore. "And now you've got me touching my face." I accused the moggy malevolently. "Don't you know, we're not supposed to touch our faces in this time of national emergency?"

In reply Mister Tibbles jumped silently to the floor and padded over to the bedroom door, before sauntering around it and out of sight.

"Bloody cat," I muttered sourly and got out of bed. I needed to inspect the damage. Mister Tibbles was waiting for me just outside my bedroom, presumably to weave himself provocatively about my ankles, to trip me on my way to the bathroom. I thumped a tired fist against Lol's bedroom door as I stumbled past. "Your bloody cat!"

I washed my hands before examining my face in the bathroom mirror. My eyes looked puffy and dry, no doubt due to the ghastly hour, combined with the two bottles of Merlot that Lol and I had polished off the night before. My nose, on the other hand, was red and scratched, like it had lost a fight to a cheese grater. *Argh! Thank god I don't have to show this in public.*

I turned from the mirror to use the toilet and caught sight of Mister Tibbles. He sat serenely on the bath mat, gazing up at me. "No, no. You ruined my lovely dream and disfigured me, you bastard cat. I am not letting you watch me take a piss. I'm not here to entertain you, Tibbles. Get out."

With an innate sense for impending danger, Mister Tibbles jumped back before my foot could make contact with him. He mewed mournfully at me before running out of the bathroom. I shut the door behind him. Firmly. *I don't know if I can take another two and a half weeks of Tibbles!*

"What's up buttercup?" Lol asked brightly as I entered the kitchen some ten minutes later. He was busy percolating coffee and unloading the dishwasher. He seemed perky, gratingly so.

"We've got to talk about Tibbles."

"That's *Mister* Tibbles, Harry," Lol corrected me, with a mischievous smirk. "Mister T doesn't like it if you don't use his proper name."

I sat down at the kitchen table. "I thought you said his proper name is 'Prince Pomander the Third?"

"No, that's his pedigree name," Lol explained and placed a tiny cup of espresso before me. "He doesn't like to brag of his royal lineage. That's why his *proper* name is Mister Tibbles. What's happened to your nose?"

"*Mister* Tibbles is what happened," I told him bluntly, just managing to stop myself from touching my nose by reflex. "Your Prince Pomander thought it quite the jolly idea to use it as a punch ball, to wake me up." I couldn't see the fluffy ratbag anywhere. "Where is he by the way?"

"Back garden, stalking squirrels." Lol handed me two Paracetamol tablets, which I took with a quick drain of my espresso cup. Molten bitterness hit the back of my throat like an express train. I coughed.

"Are you sure you haven't got the lurg?" Lol asked suspiciously and gave the kitchen table top the once over with a handy disinfectant wipe. Handy packets of wipes were strategically placed in each room of Lol's house. He'd been following the spread of the virus since the start of the year, via a financial blog he subscribed to. With some foresight, he'd been gradually gathering essentials before stockpiling suddenly became all the rage.

"Yes, I'm sure," I replied sullenly. "I wouldn't mind a regular coffee though. One that doesn't make me cough. You know, with plenty of milk and two sugars."

"Then help yourself. *Mi casa es tu casa*, Harry," Lol told me with a smile. He pulled a fleece jacket on over his lycra cycling garb and downed his espresso.

"You going out?" I asked innocently.

Lol put his cycle helmet on. "Well, seeing as you found it necessary to wake me up so early, H, I thought I'd take advantage of the beautiful morning and clear roads. Would you like to join me on a cycle ride?"

It was a token offer; Lol knew and I knew it; exercise and me are barely nodding acquaintances.

I got up and put the kettle on. "No, I think I'll go and do a set of stretch and surf in the front room."

Lol raised a quizzical eyebrow.

"By utilizing your sofa for maximum support," I explained, whilst loading a coffee cup with heaped teaspoons of instant Columbian and sugar, "I will be stretching out vigorously, with my coffee, to watch breakfast telly, followed by a session of riding the waves of the internet."

"And no need to change out of your sleep attire. Excellent! Well, make sure you don't over exert yourself. I shouldn't be gone longer than an hour." Lol opened the back door to a stream of early morning sunshine. "Maybe two. Do you want me to leave this open for Mister Tibbles?"

The sun may be shining but the air had a distinctly chilly feel to it. "No, I'll let the Prince of Pommels back in when he's finished terrorising the local wildlife." I shivered and pulled my dressing gown around me tighter. "Go! The draught is freezing."

Lol made to kiss me on the cheek but stopped himself short. "This corona business is just too weird, Harry," he whispered sadly, close to my ear.

"I know, Lol," I whispered back. We stood there for a second, not touching, but feeling the weight of our previously tactile existence fill the space between us. "Go on, go and get your daily permitted exercise."

Lol left and I finished making my coffee before settling down in front of the gogglebox. I started flicking through the channels:

squeaky clean sofa people looking solemn on BBC1; pernickety house buyers searching for their dream home on Two; Piers Morgan indulging in a bout of hissy-fitting on ITV; and on Channel Four, a careworn repeat of 'Cheers'. *Jesus fuck! What a load of crap. No thanks!*

I switched the telly off and opened my laptop. Oh, how I missed work. Not the people so much as the busyness and structure of the day. Working from home is all well and good when there's *actual* work to do, but since the Fat Kontroller had decided to furlough the business in the short-term, there wasn't very much *for* me to do. I felt redundant.

What I needed was a project, something to keep me occupied or I might end up going stark staring mad. A sudden, fearful notion gripped me: what if I started to miss Shazza, F.A. Kontrell's mouthy receptionist and bane of my working life? I mentally shuddered. *Get a grip*, I chastised myself. *Purge that image, Harry. Time to work up a sweat.*

A soft thump on the front room window, diverted my attention away from the 'Hot Russian Babes Twerking Workout' YouTube video on my laptop screen. Mister Tibbles, bane of my lockdown life, sat on the outside ledge, peering in. *Oh no, I forgot to let the cat in,* I mentally whined.

"Go round to the back," I shouted. Mister Tibbles didn't move, except for his eyes, which gave a lazy blink.

I contemplated ignoring him; that generally works with Shazza. Lol, however, would never forgive me, though, if anything happened to his beloved and extremely valuable cat. Reluctantly, I put the laptop on the floor, sighed and got up off the sofa.

"Okay, I'm coming," I called and opened the front door. Apart from a chorus of bird song, there seemed no other sign of life in the street outside.

Mister Tibbles wasn't sitting on the front window ledge; the annoying furball was nowhere to be seen. I leaned out and scanned the empty road. "Come along Mister Tibbles. Breakfast," I called sweetly. I expected to feel the soft rush of fur against my bare feet, but all I felt was a chilly, spring gust of wind on my face. "Tibbles?"

Keeping the front door ajar with my left foot, I stepped forward for a better view of the street. I was totally unprepared for the warm squelch I felt under my right heel, nor for the crunch of small bones.

"Argh!"

I lifted my leg with disbelief. A flattened and decidedly dead mouse clung to the bottom of my foot, held in place by its blood and guts. Only its tail moved, which fluttered gently in the breeze.

"ARGHHH!!!"

I hopped outside, toward the patch of lawn at the front of Lol's house; I had to wipe the foul remains off my being. "Ew, ew, EWWww! Oh My God! That is so disgusting!"

The mouse peeled off easily and lay discarded among the dewy blades, but I continued to scrape my heel and foot through the wet grass, round and around the lawn, determined to remove any rodent residue. My mind shrieked in disgust, *Unclean! Unclean!*

Miaow.

Mister Tibbles sat on the front step, watching my demented circling with a look of feline bemusement.

"Tibbles!" I rushed toward him but, sensing the murder in my heart, Mister Tibbles quickly scarpered back inside the house. "TIBBLES, NO!"

Too late. In his eagerness to escape, Mister Tibbles bumped the edge of the door with his hightailing. I watched in horror as the front door swung tantalizingly to and fro, before the wind grabbed it and brought it to a close with a *click.*

"NOOO!!!"

I stopped in my tracks, and for a split second the birds ceased their conversations and the wind dropped. There was only silence, complete silence, and I felt as if the eyes of the Universe were upon me. I stood there, utterly alone, wearing only my pyjamas, a dressing gown and some dead mouse. Then from one of the trees that lined the suburban street I heard the sound of a crow caw. To my ears it sounded like a guffaw.

A flicker of smokey grey movement caught my attention from the corner of my eye. Inside the house, Mister Tibbles had jumped up onto the front room window sill and was prowling along it, beating the glass pane with his tail.

You are so dead! I banged on the window with my fists.

Mister Tibbles didn't flinch. He meowed and leapt to the floor, before strutting over to the sofa, where he curled up in the comfy spot that until recently *I'd* been happily occupying. Seemingly ignorant of my impotent knocking, Mister Tibbles then cocked his back leg above his head and set about licking his balls.

"I'm gonna get you," I growled menacingly at the cat.

For the birds too, it appeared entertainment time was over as they went back to their noisy discussions. Not to be left out, a stream of cold air whistled past, stinging my still tender shnozz and flapping the ends of my dressing gown. I tried the front door but it was shut tight. I inspected the bottom of my foot to make sure it was mouse-free and wondered what the hell I was going to do until Lol returned. I hoped to fuck that he'd thought to take a key with him.

Did he lock the back door when he left? Lol had closed the back door, but had he locked it? I wave of hope surged through me: *Maybe I can get in through the back!*

As befitting his status of local branch bank manager, Lol's home was a modest, three bedroom terrace house. The houses either side of his were semi-detached and next to one was a side alley that led to Lol's back garden. Not wanting to track dirt into his pristine abode, Lol always used the passage to access his house when he went out cycling. I could get to his garden! Even if Lol had locked the back door, at least I could get off the street. I hadn't seen anybody walk by yet, but that was no guarantee that there wouldn't be any passersby. I decided to go for it.

Fortified with a plan of action, I belted my dressing gown tight and sprinted out of the front garden and onto the street, passing the neighbour's house until I reached the entrance to the side alley. Not being a cyclist, I'd never used the entrance before, so my heart sank when I saw the 6ft wood gate blocking the entrance. It rattled and creaked when I pushed at it but the gate wouldn't open. *Locked! Shit! I'll have to climb over it.*

With my right hand grabbing the top of the gate, I climbed up onto the neighbour's low garden wall adjacent to it. *Now, if I can just get my leg over...*

"Wot you doin?"

I froze at the sound of the voice coming from behind me.

"Yeah, wot you up to lady? You tryna break in?" a second voice, chimed in.

Oh great! Company!

I turned my head and saw two boys loitering on the street, staring at me. They were dressed in the ubiquitous teenage uniform of the day: hoodies, jeans, trainers, insolence.

"Kind of, yes," I said climbing off the wall to face them. "I've got locked out of my house."

The two boys looked at each other and then back at me. "Figures," the taller of the two boys said. "That's the wrong gear to wear for breakin' into 'ouses."

"Yeah, no gloves, no shoes. That's like trailin' your DNA shit everywhere, innit?" the second boy confirmed.

Oh God. Idiots. I shrugged my shoulders. "Well, quite."

The boys turned away and conferred for a moment. I waited patiently for them to finish, acutely aware of the ridiculousness of my situation.

Eventually the taller boy spoke. "You wanna boost?"

"Yeah, lady. You wanna boost?"

Oh God. Stereo idiots. Despite my misgivings, I decided to accept their offer. By now all I wanted to do is get inside and have a hot bath. "Yes, please. That would be lovely, thank you."

The boys approached me and the taller idiot crouched down in front of the gate with his hands held out in front of him, fingers interlocked. "So how come you got locked out then?"

"Yeah, how come?" came his echo.

I placed my left foot on the outcupped hands and grabbed the top of the gate with both hands. "That's not really any business of yours, is it?"

The fingers under my foot unlaced and it slammed to the floor. "Oww!"

The crouching idiot look up at me from beneath his hood. "Do you want our 'elp?"

"Yeah, do ya?" the second idiot asked from behind his mobile phone.

"Hold on, are you filming this?"

The first idiot stood up, towering over me. "See it's like this. We can get stuff from school for doing good works. Like vouchers for stuff. Microsoft points for the X-Box-"

"Yeah, X-Box points."

"And other things," the taller idiot continued, "But we have to be able to prove it. We've gotta have evidence of our good works, see?"

"Yeah, we gotta provide the evidence."

I was fuming but not really in a position to argue: I *did* need their help. I inspected the bottom of my foot and rubbed the gravel and grit embedded in it. "Okay, I'll tell you. But swap places with me so I can use my other foot."

I took a deep breath and addressed the phone camera. "Hello. My name is Harry Egg. I've been locked out of my friend Lol's house, where I'm staying for lockdown, by Prince Pomander the Third, and these two lovely chaps are going help me get back in."

"Wait, who's Prince Pom... Pom whatever?" the camera idiot asked. *Ha! You're not just an echo*, I thought, *but you're still an idiot.*

"Prince Pomander. The Third. He's a cat, also known as Mister Tibbles and he left a dead mouse on the doorstep for me this morning."

"Nasty!" the taller idiot said, crouching down.

"Yeah, nasty!"

"Very nasty indeed." I placed my right foot in the crouching idiot's hands, grabbed the top of the gate and lightly bounced on my standing leg. "You should have seen the blood and guts squirt out everywhere when I trod on it."

"No way! What foot?" camera idiot asked.

I pushed down hard with my right foot on crouching idiot's hands and bounced up. With a mighty heave, I pulled myself up onto the top of the gate. "The one he's holding."

"WHAA?!" Crouching idiot sprang to his feet forcefully and propelled me up and over the gate. "Nah, nah, nah. Stop filming!"

I lay flat on the ground in a daze. I could hear the boys arguing on the other side of the gate. I didn't care, I just wanted to get up and back to the house. I raised myself up into a sitting position and fought back tears.

Camera idiot's head and phone appeared over the gate. "Hey lady, you alright?"

Am I alright? I didn't think anything was broken except my pride. "Yes, fine thank you," I replied, getting to my feet and putting on a brave face. "No bones broken."

"That was wicked! I've never seen anyone fly so high!" camera idiot said enthusiastically.

"You're welcome." I turned and trailing my hand along the neighbour's high wooden fence to keep me steady, started to hobble along the alley. "And tell your friend to wash his hands."

A second gate prevented direct access to Lol's back garden, but this one wasn't so high. I would have barged it down if I'd had to, but managed to scramble over it. At last, I was in the safety of the back garden. Whereas the street was bathed in the shadow of the house, the back garden suffered no deficit of sunlight. The grass looked green and lush, sparkling with diamonds as the dew drops amplified the light, and only the gentlest of breezes caused Lol's saffron headed daffodils to bob as I passed. *It's really nice out here*, I thought. *I should have just sat out here this morning.*

I reached the back door, grabbed the handle and turned. *Please God, please God, please God.*

The door swung open. *Hallelujah!*

"Harry." Lol was opening the back gate and wheeling his bicycle into the garden. He looked athletic and ruddy. *The bastard!*

"Hello Lol. How was your ride? Busy out there?"

"Yeah, it was great. Hardly any traffic." Lol leaned his bike up against the wall of the house. "You look dreadful, Harry. Are you alright?"

"Yes, I'm fine," I said, stepping over the door threshold and into the kitchen. "I'm going to have a long, hot bath. You can come up and sit with me if you like and I'll tell you all about it." I paused. "Mister Tibbles is *not* invited."

What happened to your nose?

Long story

Shazza sent me the video of you and the 2 lads helping you over the gate.

Did she.

Says you're trending on Twitter with #WashYourHands

I know

Glad you're keeping everyone's spirits up. Only a couple of weeks to go. Keep well. xx

 Text Message

Now Hiring

Daniel Royer

Betty and Juanita sipped iced coffee on the patio of Latte Lair. It was Monday morning, and the sun shined brightly. Rush hour traffic buzzed around them. The two women, longtime friends, were in their late twenties, and it was their Monday morning ritual to sip coffee and chat at Latte Lair before their separate workdays began. Betty worked at a smoothie shop, and Juanita worked as a custodian at a middle-school. Their Monday morning coffee-chat topics, while often involving boys, nail polish, and celebrity gossip, were never complete without complaining about their jobs, and the eternal hope of acquiring better ones. This Monday morning's coffee-chat was no different. Juanita the custodian scanned the classified advertisements while Betty the smoothie operator told stories of the smoothie business.

"… So I give the lady her spinach-banana smoothie, she takes one sip and tells me it sucks. So I tell her that any smoothie with spinach in it is going to suck. That's how it is. You order a spinach smoothie because it's healthy, not because it tastes good. Then she says that maybe I just don't know how to make good smoothies. Are you kidding me? I've been making smoothies for *five* years. Believe me, *no one* can make a spinach smoothie taste good. It's been tried for ages. Can't be done. So then the lady wants a strawberry-banana smoothie instead. Now, a strawberry-banana I can do. Strawberry-bananas are easy, rookie stuff. If you can't make a good strawberry-banana smoothie, then you need to get out of the smoothie game! The cornerstone of our industry is strawberry-banana."

"I hate when the students leave their banana peels on the ground," said Juanita the custodian, still scanning the classifieds. "Also their cigarette butts.'

"So I go back," continued Betty, "and make the lady her strawberry-banana smoothie. The problem is, and this happens sometimes, I forget to put the lid on the blender. Now there's smoothie all over me and the floor."

"Smoothie is very hard to clean up," said Juanita. "You have to mop it up right away, or you have ants. With ants you have a whole new set of problems. I also don't like sweeping up sunflower seeds."

"Sometimes I don't know if the smoothie business is worth it," said Betty, sighing. "The pay is lousy and the stress is great. I would love to get out of the smoothie business, but in today's bleak economic climate, employers won't even *consider* you without a college degree and lots of experience. And what's *my* experience? Five years of mixing and blending smoothies! Now, my smoothies are the best, no doubt about it, but so what? Where does *that* get me?" Betty sipped her coffee. "But at least the smoothie business has some perks."

"What are the perks?"

"I get free smoothies on my lunch breaks."

"I often keep the change I find when sweeping the hallways."

Betty leaned towards Juanita, almost whispering. "But between you and me Juanita, I think all these free smoothies are giving me bathroom problems. Do you know what I mean?"

"I'm sure I do. The leopard-spots those students leave in the toilet bowls are really hard to clean. Also, sometimes they flush cherry bombs down the toilet. That is also hard to clean."

Suddenly, an advertisement in the classifieds caught Juanita's eye. She read it. She read it again. She grabbed Betty's hand. "Betty, I think this is a position that sounds perfect for you!"

Juanita pointed to the advertisement.

BREWBONE FINANCES
NOW HIRING HEDGE FUND MANAGER
MINIMUM 5 YEARS EXPERIENCE MANDATORY

Mr. Brewbone was the chief financial officer of Brewbone Finances. He was wrapping up an interview for the all important hedge fund manager position. The individual who undertook this position would be responsible for the financial investments of a group of prestigious clients that included, among others, an oil tycoon, a railroad baron, and a United States Senator, equaling close to one hundred million dollars in capital. Mr. Brewbone would have to be very careful in filling this position.

The subject of the interview was Davey Hudak, a twenty year employee of Brewbone Finances and the current financial planner. Davey's credentials were impeccable. In addition to a Finance Degree in which he had graduated *summa cum laude*, Davey Hudak had extensive experience in commercial banking and corporate finance. He had worked as Mr. Brewbone's top financial planner for the last six years, and his personnel record was pristine. In truth, Davey Hudak's interview was more of a formality. He was immensely qualified, and Mr. Brewbone had every intention of promoting him.

There was only one problem. Without exception, all of Brewbone Finances' top positions were filled by men. Rumors of sexism plagued the investment firm, Mr. Brewbone himself being the subject of many such complaints. Brewbone Finances had recently settled a wrongful termination suit filed by a disgruntled female receptionist, and the previous hedge fund manager was forced to resign after he had gotten said receptionist pregnant. The lawyers in town were starting to circle Brewbone Finances.

Mr. Hendershot, the firm's corporate attorney, had told Mr. Brewbone that if at all possible, the hedge fund manager position should be filled by a woman. They needed to feed the litigious sharks something, *anything*. Mr. Brewbone considered this during the lengthy interview process, but in truth, he felt that none of the female applicants were particularly qualified, certainly not as qualified as Davey Hudak.

"Well, Davey," said Mr. Brewbone, extending his hand, "barring some unforeseen circumstance, the hedge fund manager position is yours."

Davey smiled, shaking Mr. Brewbone's hand. "May I ask, how many more interviews do you have left?"

"Just one," said Mr. Brewbone, scanning the paperwork. He picked up the final resume. He almost laughed. "And I wouldn't worry about it… So, put some champagne on ice, and you'll hear from me by the end of the day."

"Yes sir. Thank you Mr. Brewbone." Davey Hudak walked out of the office.

Mr. Brewbone bit into an apple. This stressful interview process left him without time for a proper lunch. He scanned the final resume.

The applicant was indeed a female, indicating five years of experience, though the particulars of that experience were vague. The phone rang. He picked it up. It was Mr. Hendershot, the corporate attorney.

"Who are you leaning towards?" asked Mr. Hendershot.

"Well, Davey, of course," said Mr. Brewbone. "He has the most experience and best qualifications."

"Have you given any more thought to what we discussed?"

"I have indeed. Truth be told, these female applicants haven't been up to snuff. Honest. And we're talking over a hundred million dollars in investment opportunities here. I'm not going to just give the position to some Jane whose only qualification is she wears a skirt."

"Of course not. And nobody's asking you to do that. I only said that, for the sake of appearances, the position ideally should be filled by a woman... who meets the qualifications of course... Tell me, how many more interviews do you have?"

"Just one. A Betty-something," said Mr. Brewbone. "She's due any time now."

"What's her deal?"

Mr. Brewbone scanned her resume again. "Five years of experience. Of what? I don't know. Her resume's a little short on some details."

"Well, if she's qualified—"

"I know, I know," said Mr. Brewbone.

"Let me finish. If she has the qualifications. Scratch that, if she even *remotely* meets the qualifications, you hire her. Understand? I like Davey as much you do, but we can't afford to continue this public relations disaster. *Or* another lawsuit."

Mr. Brewbone's intercom buzzed. He pushed the button. "Yes?"

"Your next interview is here," said his receptionist.

"Thank you. Send her in."

"Mind if I listen in on this?" asked Mr. Hendershot.

"Please do," said Mr. Brewbone. He put the telephone on speaker mode.

There was a knock on the door. "Come in," said Mr. Brewbone.

A girl in her twenties entered.

Mr. Brewbone stood, extending his hand. "You must be Betty. I'm Mr. Brewbone, CFO of Brewbone Finances. Have a seat please."

Betty sat. Mr. Brewbone studied her. She sat calmly with hands folded in her lap. She exuded confidence.

"First off Betty, what is your educational background?"

"I'm a high school graduate."

"I see," said Mr. Brewbone. Already he knew that this applicant lacked the qualifications to fill the position, which required a strong educational foundation. "And your previous job experience…?"

"I have worked for the last five years at a smoothie shop."

"And what are your duties at this smoothie shop?" This question was a formality. Mentally, he had already closed the book on Betty the smoothie girl. For the sake of appearances, he would finish the interview just to satisfy Mr. Hendershot.

"My duties consist of chopping, blending and smoothing a melange of fruit to a perfect cup of perfection, while investing in our customers' health and well-being." Mr. Brewbone thought that this was a very odd way saying that she put fruit in a blender and pushed a button.

"Do you have any financial experience?"

"Yes I do. My duties require me to give out exact change to our customers, or clients if you will. I am responsible for all the money in my register—the entire pool. My manager, who I have listed on my resume, will vouch for this."

This farce had gone on long enough, decided Mr. Brewbone. "I am sorry Betty. But I'm afraid you don't meet the qualifications for this position."

Betty was visibly taken aback. "Mr. Brewbone, I think you're contradicting yourself. I have a copy of your job posting, and I believe I'm a perfect match for the position's requirements as you have stated them."

"Excuse me? I don't understand," said Mr. Brewbone. *What was this girl talking about?*

Betty pulled a folded piece of paper out of her pocket. She unfolded it, placing it on the table. Mr. Brewbone picked it up. It was indeed the job listing he had posted in the local newspaper. He read.

BREWBONE FINANCES
NOW HIRING HEDGE FUND MANAGER
MINIMUM 5 YEARS EXPERIENCE MANDATORY

Brewbone Finances is seeking applicants to fill our hedge fund manager position. Applicants must have an *education*, and have a minimum of *five years of financial experience*. Duties include *chopping* wasted overhead, *blending* a *melange* of stocks, bonds, and discretionary funds, and *smoothing* things over with our well-to-do clientele. The position will make *investments* involving our clients' financial *well-being*. Hedge fund manager will be *responsible* for the *entire pool* of investment capital. Experience mandatory in this regard—*previous employer must vouch for this*. Hedge fund manager's financial results *must bear much fruit*.

Mr. Brewbone went slack-jawed. The job posting fell from his hand, floating to the desk. Betty picked it up. "As we have already discussed, I have a high school *education*, and *five years* of experience, including *financial* experience. My current duties include *chopping*, *blending*, and *smoothing*. For *five years* I have looked after our customers', or clients' *well-being*, including the well-being of their *finances*, as I have short-changed no one. My *manager* can *vouch* for all of this. Oh, and of course, working in the smoothie industry for *five years*, I have *beared much fruit*."

Mr. Brewbone was speechless. He stammered.

"Let me help you, Mr. Brewbone. The way I see it, I match the position's qualifications perfectly. It would seem disingenuous to state otherwise, and if I were not granted the position, I'd have to assume it is because I am a woman, of which I see very few at this boys' club you call 'Brewbone Finances.' I'm sure there's plenty of lawyers in town who would agree with me."

Mr. Brewbone sat, dazed. Betty got up, extending her hand. Mr. Brewbone shook it numbly. "I'll expect a call from you, by say, 4 o'clock?" said Betty. "Law offices start closing shortly after that."

Betty walked towards the door. She stopped suddenly, turning. "And by the way, contrary to popular belief, I make even spinach smoothies taste good." And with that, she walked out of the office, closing the door behind her.

Mr. Brewbone cleared his throat. "Did you get all that?" he asked, directing his question to the speaker on the telephone.

Mr. Hendershot said, "I did."

"And?"

"You must hire her."

Of course Davey Hudak was furious. Who wouldn't be? He quit upon hearing the news. He called Mr. Brewbone all sorts of names. He even threatened a lawsuit. Mr. Hendershot told Mr. Brewbone not to worry about Davey's legal threat. Mr. Hendershot assured Mr. Brewbone that with the hiring of the girl, they were on solid legal ground. The town's litigious sharks would be pacified.

Betty, who just yesterday was making smoothies for a living, would fill the hedge fund manager position the following Monday, overseeing an investment pool of one hundred million dollars in capital for, among others, an oil tycoon, a railroad baron, and a United States Senator. In the meantime, Mr. Brewbone had to start interviewing for Davey Hudak's old position, that of financial planner.

Mr. Brewbone sat in his office, his fingers poised over the computer keyboard as he prepared to compose the job posting for the financial planner position. He needed to be very careful with his words this time. His investment firm could not afford another smoothie-girl fiasco.

Mr. Brewbone knew just what to say. He began to write.

The following Monday morning, Juanita the custodian sat alone on the patio outside of Latte Lair. Betty would no longer be able to join her for the Monday ritual, as she had started her new job. Juanita sipped coffee, scanning the classified advertisements. She had been working for a long time as a janitor at a middle-school, and she was starting to get tired of it. For six years she had been cleaning, mopping, and sweeping the debris of middle-schoolers. She handled everything, from big messes, to discarded banana peels. She even had to deal with the money she found on the ground.

She thought of Betty. She was so proud of Betty and her new job. She was also a little bit jealous. If Betty was able to get a new job, then why not Juanita? She told herself that she just needed to be patient, and wait to see a ship on the horizon—and when she saw that ship, well, she would hop aboard. She continued to scan the classifieds. An advertisement caught her eye.

BREWBONE FINANCES
NOW HIRING FINANCIAL PLANNER
MINIMUM SIX YEARS EXPERIENCE NECESSARY

Brewbone Finances is seeking applicants to fill our financial planner position. Our investment firm has slipped on a figurative *banana peel*, and has a pretty *big mess* to *clean*. Applicants must have *six years of experience* in dealing with *money*, as well as *mopping* up the damage of previous employees who, frankly, have acted like *middle-schoolers*. As Brewbone Finances has had a tumultuous experience with lawsuits and accusations, the financial planner's duties will sometimes include *sweeping* things under the proverbial rug.

Juanita circled the advertisement. Her ship had come in.

The Car and the Redhead

Daniel Royer

"Roger Barton," announced the loud speaker. "Please see Mr. Rufus in his office."

Barton wondered why the sales manager needed to see him so early in the morning. He looked at his watch. Wrong. It was afternoon. Barton cupped his hand to his mouth, checking his breath. Booze breath. He popped in two mints to mask the scent. The young salesman examined himself in the reflection of his computer monitor. The results were not pretty. Blood-shot eyes, mussed hair, and a wrinkled shirt with wine stains and cat hair all over it.

The previous evening had been a rough one for Barton. The redhead that worked at the cookie shop in the mall had rejected him. Again. She said she didn't date broke guys that lived in their parents' garages. She said she didn't date losers.

Barton applied eye drops, ran a comb through his mop, and shifted his tie askew to cover the wine stain. He popped in two more breath mints for good luck, and headed over to the sales office. Again he wondered why he was being summoned to old man Rufus's office.

"You needed to see me boss?" said Barton as he walked in.

"Yeah, Barton, take a seat will you." The young salesman sat across from Mr. Rufus at his desk. Mr. Rufus was a fat old man with pasty skin. His jowls shook when he spoke. With thick fingers, Mr. Rufus turned a page in a file. Barton noticed that the file was his own.

"Do you know why we're here Barton?"

"Not a clue boss."

Mr. Rufus sighed, turned another page in the file. "You've been late almost every day this month. Sometimes you don't show up at all. You sleep at your desk, your attitude's rotten, and you smell like a wino. Your customer reviews are terrible, and we're currently the defendant in a class-action sexual harassment suit because of you. And I'll be honest, all these things I could live with if you were making sales... Tell me, when was the last time you sold a car, Barton?"

Barton shook his head—damned if he knew.

"Six months," said Mr. Rufus, examining the file. Barton actually thought it had been longer. "It's been six months since your last sale. That is unacceptable at Rufus Cars. At Rufus Cars, we expect our salesmen to sell cars! Lots of the them!" Barton sighed. Rufus Cars had really high standards that way.

"I'll try to do better boss."

"That's not good enough Barton. I've given you a long leash because of your old man. But I've taken that as far as I can go."

Roger Barton's dad, Barton Senior, had been a salesman at Rufus Cars back when old man Rufus was merely middle-aged Rufus. Barton Senior was the greatest salesman Rufus Cars ever had. Some of the veteran salesmen still hanging around the donut room said that Barton Senior could sell a car to anyone, and on one occasion, had even sold a car to a man with no arms, no legs, and no money. Also the man was blind. Month after month, Barton Senior was at the top of the sales charts. To put it simply, the man was a rock star at Rufus Cars.

But all that prestige came crashing down during the gas crises of the Carter Administration in the 1970's. Over night, people started bicycling to work and walking to the grocery store. Suddenly, the man who sold automobiles to *everyone* had trouble selling to *anyone*. Barton Senior turned to drink and women. He got depressed. Night after night, the washed-up car salesman got into bar-fights, often receiving midnight dental work. After years of this, Mrs. Barton Senior became fed up. She made him sleep on the couch. And one day, Barton Senior found himself parked in his garage with a hose in the tailpipe. Due to the petroleum shortage at the time, the car ran out of gas before he could finish the job.

Barton Senior now worked as a flunky at a gas station. The man was a disgrace.

"What do you need me to do boss?" asked young Barton.

"I need you to make a sale. Today. Or you're out on your duff. A loser. Just like your old man."

Jimmy Shiner stepped onto the lot of Rufus Cars. The twenty-five year old kid had done his homework. All the top bloggers and podcast hosts had said that the Goat 100 was the car to get. The vehicle was dependable, affordable, and safe. Jimmy Shiner didn't care about flash or muscle like the Antelope 200 or the Python 300. He only cared about price, reliability, and the hand of a cute redhead that worked at the cookie store in the mall. Unfortunately, Shiner's budget was pretty limited because he worked part-time at the sunglass hut, right across from the cookie store. The kid was looking for a deal. He had been driving an old Smokestack for several years, and it was time for a new vehicle. The cookie girl wouldn't date guys who drove Smokestacks. She refused to go out with Jimmy Shiner. She said he was a loser. Perhaps a Goat 100 would change her mind.

Shiner was a little nervous because this would be his first car purchase without his mom's co-signature. He wanted, what the top bloggers called, a primo deal. Quite simply, he just didn't want to be one of those chumps who made a mistake. Shiner walked through the lot scanning the cars, pretending he knew what he was doing. His favorite podcast host suggested to frown a lot and cross your arms, just like those wily deal-makers did in the movies. A salesman approached Shiner. Shiner tried to look confidant and shrewd. The salesman had cat hair on his slacks and a wine stain on his shirt. He was young, like Shiner.

"Hi ho. Welcome to Rufus Cars," said the young salesman, smiling. "Roger Barton's the name."

"I'm Jimmy Shiner, and I don't want no guff, or I'll walk right out of here!" The top blogs always said to talk like a tough-guy.

"No guff here Jimmy, only quality cars. What kind are you looking for?"

"A Goat 100, or I'll walk out of here!"

Roger Barton continued to smile, but this news about the Goat distressed him. Rufus Cars was sold out of Goats. The competent salesmen at the dealership had already closed on all of them. The Goats sold extremely well because they were so reliable and economical. All the top podcasts were raving about them. In all seriousness, Goats were wonderful vehicles and Roger Barton wished he could own one himself. He really needed a sale today though— time to turn on the old Barton salesman charm.

"I *could* offer you the Goat 100—we have plenty of them—but you seem like a nice kid, so I'll be straight with you. The Goat 100 is bad."

"But I heard that the Goat was good. They say it's dependable."

"It's not. They break down all the time."

"But they say it's affordable."

"It's not. The Goat will cost you a lot of money."

"Well, I also heard that it's safe."

"It's not. The Goats catch on fire for no reason at all. I'm a straight-shooter Jimmy. I *could* sell you an expensive car that'll break down before you make it out of the lot and will eventually kill you, but I care about my customers. That's why I always try to steer them to the Antelope 200..." Barton scanned the lot, settling his gaze on the most expensive vehicle. "... But I can tell that you're not just a regular customer. For you, I suggest the Python 300."

Shiner whistled. "Thank you for your honesty. Tell me about the Python 300... or I'll walk right out of here!"

The Python 300 was an expensive hot rod favored by race car drivers. The Python 300 had a good reputation for winning. Unfortunately, it had another reputation that wasn't so good: it was also known for randomly exploding. Just a week prior, a famous race car driver had died in a fiery crash after his Python blew up on a race track before flipping into the grandstand and killing a lot of people. The crash photos were all over the tabloids. The widow was suing. The Python was currently involved in a massive recall. In addition, the Python 300 had no longevity, no safety features, and since it was indeed a race car, no headlights. It also had horrible gas mileage—roughly a mile to the gallon—and required only expensive premium rocket fuel that no gas station even offered. Barton needed to spin this.

He led Shiner over to a cherry-red Python. It was the most expensive model on the lot. There were flames on the sides. Jimmy Shiner touched the flame decals. It was a beautiful car. He could imagine himself driving it with a cute redhead in the passenger seat. Roger Barton walked laps around the vehicle as he spoke.

"Simply put, Jimmy, the Python is the best car ever made."

"What can it do?" asked Shiner.

"It would be easier to say what it *can't* do... *Nothing*."

"Is it dependable?"

"Yes. You'll drive it for decades."

"Is it affordable?"

"Yes. It's so cheap."

108

"Is it safe?"

"The safest. No one has ever gotten hurt in it."

"How's the gas mileage?"

"Really good."

"How much horsepower has it got?" Shiner had no idea what this meant, but all the top bloggers said to say it.

"About a thousand. I'm telling you Jimmy, the Python 300 is the car for you."

Jimmy Shiner considered this. This was great news. The Python 300 sure sounded like a swell car. Also, the Goat seemed like a real piece of garbage. A garbage-car certainly was not going to woo a beautiful young lady. Shiner thought back to the magazine articles he had read. The articles said that it was usually a good idea to test-drive a vehicle before purchasing it.

"I think I'd like to take this out for a test-drive."

This was the last thing Roger Barton wanted. If he were to allow the Python to be test-driven, the car was liable to break down, run out of gas, or possibly explode. He might even lose the sale. Barton thought of old man Rufus's ultimatum, and the sweet redhead at the mall. He could not blow this deal.

"Normally, I encourage my customers to test-drive our cars. But the Python is so trustworthy, that you have my personal guarantee that you'll love it. Frankly, a test-drive would insult my honor."

Shiner certainly didn't want to insult anybody's honor. But he remembered the blogs he had read. They said that car salesmen sometimes were not completely truthful. This Barton guy seemed on the level, but Shiner needed to make sure.

"I think I'm going to have to insist on that test-drive."

Barton sighed. "I'm going to be totally honest, Jimmy. You've just hurt my feelings. I gave you my *personal* guarantee. I don't give that out to most customers. I thought you were special."

"I'm so sorry," said Shiner. "It's just that there's this girl that works near me. She's got dimples and everything. She thinks I'm a loser. I just thought that maybe if I got a new car, she'd give me a shot."

Roger Barton was actually touched by this. He thought of the sweet redhead at the mall. It appeared he and Shiner were in a similar situation. He smiled. "Well Jimmy, I've got some good news for you... Babes love Pythons."

"They do?"

"Absolutely. Old babes, young babes, skanks, redheads, whatever your thing is… Believe me, Jimmy, if you purchase this vehicle today, you'll be making out with a babe in the backseat by sundown."

This was all the information that Jimmy Shiner needed. He stuck out his hand. "I'll take a Python."

"You've made a wise decision today, friend. Let's get the paperwork started in the donut room. We've got the ones with sprinkles."

It was twenty minutes later. Shiner was seated across from Barton at his desk. A box of donuts rested between them. "How about another donut, Jimmy?" asked Barton.

"Just one more," said Shiner, reaching for a fritter. "I've got to keep trim to get a kiss from that cutie. All the magazines say that beautiful young ladies don't go for guys with spare-tires. They prefer six-packs."

"What they really prefer are Python 300s," said Barton.

The boys laughed. Shiner chewed on his fritter, thinking back to the blogs he had read. They always said that price was one of the most important things. They suggested to find out the price before signing. "How much does the Python cost?"

Barton had anticipated this question—in fact, he had been thinking about the answer to the question since he first saw the kid on the lot. The manufacturer's suggested retail price listed the Python at two hundred thousand dollars. Barton needed to play this very carefully.

He cleared his throat. "A million."

Shiner whistled. "I don't think that is in my budget. I work part-time at a sunglass hut in the mall. Do you have any deals or coupons?"

"I don't know. My sales manager is a hard case. Let's see what he says." Barton called over old man Rufus.

The sales manager waddled over to them.

"Mr. Rufus, meet Jimmy Shiner. He wants a Python."

"Excellent choice, young man," said Rufus, shaking Shiner's hand.

Barton spoke. "The problem is that Mr. Shiner works at a sunglass hut in the mall. As you know of course, a Python costs a million dollars, and that price is a little high for him. Do you think we can help him out?"

"Hmm, I don't know," said Mr. Rufus, scratching his chin. "There's not much I can do about that sales price."

"But Jimmy's heart is really set on that Python. There's this girl with dimples he's got a crush on. Do you think we could maybe give him a deal... say, for only *half* a million...?"

"Half a million!" exclaimed Rufus. "That's just giving it away!"

"I know it's going to cost us money, but Jimmy here is a good kid. It's the right thing to do."

Rufus sighed. "Our shareholders will have our duffs for this, but maybe you're right." He smiled. "Mr. Shiner, you have a deal at half a million. Take it. It's yours."

"Thanks Mr. Rufus," said Jimmy Shiner. Mr. Rufus walked away.

"The old man really likes you," said Barton, smiling.

"I know I'm getting a great deal and all," said Shiner, shifting in his seat, "but half a million is still a little steep for me."

"Well, with a down-payment, your trade-in, and some low financing, you should be able to swing it."

"Maybe I can work some extra shifts at the sunglass hut until it's paid off."

"Sure you can. Now what kind of payment are you able to put down?"

Jimmy Shiner fidgeted. He had heard of down-payments before. All the blogs talked about them. The problem was that he didn't have any money to put down. He did, however, have a pretty good gig at a sunglass hut, and that gig had some perks.

Shiner reached into his pocket, pulling out a crumbled piece of paper. He placed it on the desk.

"What's this?" asked Barton, picking it up.

"That is a voucher for a pair Sweet Rays." Sweet Rays were the hottest new sunglasses on the market. All the top movie stars were wearing them at premiers. They were selling for thousands of dollars. Shiner had stolen the voucher from the sunglass hut.

Roger Barton studied the voucher. He loved Sweet Rays. His favorite rock star had worn them in his latest music video. Barton thought of the redhead at the mall. He could just imagine himself strutting up to the cookie stand wearing a new pair of Sweet Rays. What girl could resist?

"Will that work as a down-payment?" asked Jimmy Shiner.

"Jimmy, this will work just fine. Now, what kind of trade-in you got for us today?"

"I got a Smokestack. It's pretty old, but it still drives well."

"Let's see how much she's worth." Barton plugged in the Smokestack's stats on the computer. The computer said Shiner's car was worth around ten grand. Smokestacks were known for retaining their value. Barton found this annoying. He would not let this stop him. "That's too bad," he said, shaking his head.

"What is it?" asked Shiner.

"Computer says your car's not worth *anything*. In fact, we have to charge you a junking fee."

"Oh no. Can you maybe ask Mr. Rufus for a discount on that junking fee?"

Barton smiled. "You know what, I don't need to ask Mr. Rufus. You're a good kid. I'm going to wave that junking fee. We'll junk that Smokestack for you for free."

"Thanks Mr. Barton."

"You bet. Now let's talk financing. Let's check your credit score."

Jimmy Shiner knew his credit score. All the top podcast hosts suggested that consumers know their credit scores. Shiner's mom payed off his credit card without fail every month. She had worked his score up to 810. Shiner knew that 810 was excellent—the most trusted podcasts said so. Jimmy's mom told him that she would stop paying off his credit card soon. He was a grownup now, and grownups pay for their own credit cards.

"My credit score is 810!" exclaimed Shiner.

Barton hated when his customers knew their credit scores. He wished all those bloggers would shut up about it. Of course, 810 was an excellent credit score. It would qualify the kid for a variety of very low APR financing. Barton needed to work his way around this.

"810, huh? That's pretty rough."

"I beg your pardon..."

"810's a rough score. I'm sorry."

"I thought 810 was good."

"It's not. It's bad. But don't worry. I'll find you some good financing." He inputted some fake numbers on the computer. "Good news, Jimmy. Looks like Rufus Cars can offer you some very low financing at only forty percent."

"Is that a good deal?" Shiner's favorite blogger said it was important to get a good deal on financing, the lower the better.

"It's a great deal. That interest is less than half—practically nothing at all."

"Then I'll take it!"

"Easy there," chuckled Barton. "Let's review this one more time." Barton thought of the redhead at the mall, and how impressed she would be at the deal he was about to make. He scanned some paperwork. He read: "We're looking at a brand new Python 300, half the MSRP at five hundred grand, a voucher for a pair of Sweet Rays, a waved junking fee for your trade-in, and very low forty percent APR financing..."

Barton slid a paper over to Shiner and held up a pen. He looked at Shiner square in the eyes, just like his old man would have done. "Now all I need you to do is sign."

Jimmy Shiner sat in his brand new Python 300. The paperwork had been signed, the hands had been shaken, and the vehicle was his. Shiner had agreed to everything Mr. Barton had offered him, except for the insurance. He worked part-time at a sunglass hut, for goodness sake—he couldn't afford *all* the perks. Shiner breathed in deeply, savoring that new-car smell. With half off the sales price and next-to-nothing financing, the car was practically free. His favorite podcast host would be proud of him. His mother would be proud of him. Maybe the cookie girl would be proud of him too. Shiner checked the fuel gauge. The Python was full of gas and waiting to be driven some place. Any place. Jimmy Shiner would go there.

"I tell you, kid. You've done good today. As long as you swing sales like that, you'll always have a place at Rufus Cars."

"Thanks old man," said Barton. He was lounging with Mr. Rufus in his office. They were drinking beer and smoking cigars with their feet up on the desk. A smoke haze wafted above their heads. Barton's commission on the deal would be tremendous. Additionally, he would be getting a new pair of Sweet Rays and a used Smokestack. Perhaps this would catch the attention of a particular redhead at the mall. Maybe he would swing by the cookie shop after he finished his beer.

Mr. Rufus handed Barton a check. Barton held it up, smiling.

"That's a lot of money for a young guy like you," said Mr. Rufus. "What you gonna spend it on?"

"Well, the first thing I'm gonna buy is an oatmeal raisin."

"Oatmeal raisin?"

"That's right. You see, there's this sweet redhead that works at the cookie shop in the mall..."

Mr. Rufus chuckled. "Oh to be a young man like you again, Barton. I remember when Mrs. Rufus was a cutie working at a malt shop. I drank a lot of vanilla shakes that summer. I had to work extra shifts on my paper-route to save up money to take her to a drive-in movie. I borrowed my old man's '57 Goat. Mrs. Rufus and I made out in the backseat all night long. I've loved babes and cars ever since. I guess that's how I got into this business." Mr. Rufus cracked open another beer, handing it to Barton.

"But seriously, Barton," continued Mr. Rufus. "Your old man would be proud of you. I remember back during the Ford Administration, your pops actually got an Amish guy to trade in his buggy for a Gazelle 400. The turbo model. What's the old man up to these days?"

"He's grease-monkeying it over at some gas station. At home he sleeps on the couch."

The boys laughed.

Jimmy Shiner cruised around town for a while. He put on his lucky pair of Sting Screens—they weren't as good as Sweet Rays, but he still looked pretty boss in them. Shiner had purchased them with his employee discount at the hut a few weeks prior. He had been waiting for a special occasion to debut them.

114

Shiner drove the streets looking for kicks. He raced a guy driving an Antelope 200. Shiner burned his ass. He also got ticketed by a cop for street-racing. Shiner ran a couple red lights, and pulled into the parking lot of a malt shop. He did some donuts in the parking lot and whistled at girls. After the security guard told him to leave, he drove over to a liquor store. Shiner purchased a dozen roses and a pack of cigarettes. He lit one up, and rolled the pack in his shirt sleeve. This was what cool guys with hot sleds did in the movies. Afterwards, he drove over to the mall.

Shiner parked beside a Smokestack that reminded him of his old car. Jimmy lit another cigarette and entered the mall. With flowers in hand, he approached the cookie store. Shiner stopped short. He saw the salesman Mr. Barton in front of the cookie shop. Mr. Barton was wearing a pair of Sweet Rays. The price tag still dangled from the frames. Mr. Barton and the redhead were leaning over the counter splitting an oatmeal raisin. She was laughing at Mr. Barton's jokes while she tossed her hair. Shiner ducked behind a hot dog cart and watched. Mr. Barton was showing the redhead a check. She giggled, and touched his bicep. She leaned over the counter for a kiss.

A security guard tapped Jimmy Shiner's shoulder. The security guard told him to put out his cigarette. Shiner back-talked the security guard a little and called him names. The security guard fingered his baton and threatened to arrest him. Shiner stubbed his cigarette out on the hot dog cart, and chucked the flowers in the mall water fountain. He decided to head home. He would tell his mom about the sweet deal he had swung.

Shiner drove home, squinting into the dark night. He had been pulled over and ticketed for driving without headlights. It was the damnedest thing, but Shiner couldn't find the button to turn them on. He would look into that later. The evening was warm, and Shiner rolled down the windows. He turned on the radio. He was almost home when he heard a rumbling sound coming from under the hood. Smoke began to pour out of it. Shiner checked his gauges. A light said he was out of gas.

Shiner pulled the car over. He saw a gas station a block away. He pushed the Python over to the gas station, and stepped inside. Shiner approached the register, and rang the bell. An old man wearing a blue jumpsuit stepped out from the back. The jumpsuit had cat hair and a wine stain on it.

"Hi ho. Welcome to Senior Gas."

Shiner lit a cigarette at the counter. "I'm Jimmy Shiner, and I don't want no guff, or I'll walk right out of here!"

"No guff here Jimmy, only quality gas. What kind are you looking for?"

"Premium rocket fuel. I got a brand new Python, and she only takes the best." Shiner pointed out the window. The old man could see the vehicle parked next to the pump. He used to sell Pythons back in the seventies.

"Premium rocket fuel, huh?" he said, scratching his chin.

"That's right. You got any?"

The old man did not have any premium rocket fuel. No one did. Except maybe NASA. He *did* have some nice regular diesel fuel though... for a premium price.

"Yeah, sure kid, I got premium rocket fuel. It'll cost you though..."

"How much?"

"Well normally it goes for a hundred bucks a gallon."

"A hundred bucks sounds pretty steep. Give me a deal, or I'll walk right out of here!"

"Whoa, easy there kid. I can tell no salesman is going to railroad *you*. Since you seem like a nice guy, I can let you have it for only fifty bucks a gallon. Any less, and I'll lose money."

"Now that sounds more like it!"

The old man smiled. "How much premium rocket fuel would you like?"

"Fill her up to the top," said Shiner.

Jimmy was reaching into his wallet, when there was an explosion outside. The entire building rattled. The ground shook and the windows shattered. A fire alarm sounded off. Jimmy Shiner screamed. The old man cursed. They looked out the window. The Python 300 was on fire. Flames were spreading towards the pumps. The pumps caught on fire, and the Python exploded again.

"Ah, never mind," said Jimmy Shiner, putting away his wallet. He walked out the door, and headed for home.

The old man shrugged. It wasn't the first sale that he had blown.

A Question of Firing

Daniel Royer

DeCarlo was called into Mr. Lee's office. Mr. Lee wore a solemn expression. DeCarlo took a seat across from him at his desk.

"The quarterly reports came in yesterday," said Mr. Lee.

"And…?" asked DeCarlo, hopefully.

Mr. Lee simply shook his head. It had been a dreadful quarter—a dreadful year in fact. Everyone at Lee Industries knew it.

"The board met this morning," said Mr. Lee. "We're going to have to… I'm sorry DeCarlo, but it has to come from your department… You're going to have to let somebody go. Today."

DeCarlo hung his head. He hated firing people. Of course he did. People did crazy things when they got fired.

"Any questions?" asked Mr. Lee.

"Who do you think would take it the best?"

"Does it matter?"

DeCarlo went to his office to think it over. This was a tricky situation. People yelled when they got fired. They threw things. DeCarlo had been called filthy names. Sometimes the filthy names were aimed at his wife. People tried to talk DeCarlo out of it. Sometimes they incorporated emotional blackmail: '*How am I going to pay my mortgage? Feed my kids?*' Why is it that everyone who gets fired has a sick wife or some hungry kids? And sometimes the craziness wasn't just confined to the office. One time DeCarlo had found that his tires were slashed. Another time his dog Muffin died under mysterious circumstances a mere twenty-four hours after firing some guy. There were ransom notes. Death threats. Weird things got left on DeCarlo's front porch and mailbox. People became unpredictable when they lost their jobs.

The key was to fire someone who wouldn't go berserk. DeCarlo needed someone mild-mannered. He reviewed his staff. There was

Bruce, of course. Bruce was pretty big though. It looked like Bruce worked out. DeCarlo had never seen Bruce act aggressively, but who knew what those biceps were capable of under the right circumstances. Bruce was out. Someone else. Well, there was Stephen. Stephen didn't seem intimidating. DeCarlo thought about this. But Stephen was always doing those office pranks. The pranks were harmless, funny even. But it took a clever and diabolical mind to successfully perform pranks. DeCarlo would hate to see what that diabolic mind could produce when it was under duress. Stephen was out too. Perhaps a female? There was Stacey. Stacey wasn't big, Stacey wasn't diabolical. Why not Stacey? Well, Stacey was sassy. DeCarlo often liked her sass. Everyone did. It charged the office atmosphere. But how easily DeCarlo could see that sass turning into venom in the right context. DeCarlo had been called some mean things during these situations over the years. He would hate to hear the vile things Stacey might have to offer him. Stacey was out.

Who did that leave? Not many more. Then DeCarlo thought of Harold. Harold wasn't big, Harold wasn't clever, Harold had no sass. Harold came to work on time every day, was polite to everyone, then Harold went home. Harold seemed ideal. DeCarlo could think of no reason that would preclude him from firing Harold.

Harold was the one.

DeCarlo picked up the phone. He dialed Mr. Lee's extension.

"Hello, Mr. Lee?... Yes, I have chosen... I will fire Harold."

There was a gentle knock on DeCarlo's office door. DeCarlo noted that Harold even *knocked* politely. DeCarlo was confident that Harold was the right choice.

Harold stepped into the office, shoulders hunched. He wore khaki pants and a lavender shirt. Harold was about as milquetoast as an employee could get. "Good morning, Mr. DeCarlo," he said.

"Good morning, Harold. Have a seat please." Harold sat, legs crossed, hands folded in his lap. DeCarlo had learned over the years to just get right down to it when it came to firing people. He also learned to have a can of mace ready. It was waiting in an open drawer just within arm's reach.

"I'm sorry, Harold, but I'm going to have to let you go. This has nothing to do with your performance. This is purely because, well, you know the company is struggling… I'm afraid that's how it is."

Harold inhaled deeply—blew out. He stood solemnly and extended his hand. "Thank you, Mr. DeCarlo. I know this must have been hard for you. I thank you for these past few years, and I wish you and the company the best of luck in the future."

DeCarlo couldn't believe what he was seeing, what he was hearing. He had been yelled at and spat on. His college diploma had been taken from the wall and torn apart. His car had been vandalized, and his dog Muffin had been butchered. Terrifying things had been mailed to him or left on his porch. DeCarlo had seen it all. But he had never seen anyone stand up, extend a hand, and actually *thank* him.

DeCarlo gratefully shook Harold's hand. Harold was turning to walk away when DeCarlo said, "And please feel free to use me as a reference in the future. I would be happy to give you one."

"That won't be necessary," said Harold.

"But you'll need my reference to secure employment elsewhere. May I ask, what are your plans?"

Harold stood erect, looking DeCarlo squarely in the face. "I'm going to kill myself."

DeCarlo reached for the mace—stopped himself. Wrong reaction. He closed the drawer. "I—what? You're going to what? Harold, you're not serious."

"I am… But it's not your fault, Mr. DeCarlo, I assure you."

But it is *my fault,* thought DeCarlo. *I'm the one firing you!* He couldn't believe what he was hearing. DeCarlo had heard some threats in his years, but this was outrageous.

"Harold, this is emotional blackmail!"

"Oh no, it's not. Just don't even worry about it, Mr. DeCarlo."

"But I'm worried, Harold. Okay? I'm worried… How are you going to… kill yourself anyway?" DeCarlo could think of no other question to ask.

"I don't know," said Harold. "Pills? Razor blade? There's an archery range near my house… I'll figure it out when I get home. Goodbye, Mr. DeCarlo. No hard feelings." Harold turned and walked towards the office door. DeCarlo could not let this happen. This was even worse than some of those ransom notes he had received in the past.

"Harold, stop!" Harold stopped just short of the door. "Don't kill yourself!"

"I'm sorry, Mr. DeCarlo, but my mind is made up."

"But, but..." Mr. DeCarlo thought back to the movies he had seen where some slick negotiator is talking someone out of jumping off a bridge. "You have so much to live for!"

"With all due respect, Mr. DeCarlo, that's easy for you to say. You have a job. I don't. Good day, sir."

DeCarlo thought quickly. Maybe he had gotten it wrong with Harold. Maybe Bruce with the muscles, or Stephen with the pranks, or Stacey with the sass would be better candidates. Before he could change his mind, he blurted, "Harold, what if you kept your job?"

"I beg your pardon?"

"You're keeping your job. I insist. Just please don't kill yourself, okay?"

"I'm sorry, Mr. DeCarlo, but I think I'm still going to kill myself."

"But why? You have your job."

"Yeah, but I'm depressed now."

"What would make you not depressed?" asked DeCarlo.

"I don't know," said Harold, scratching his head.

"Money?" asked DeCarlo. "How about more money?"

"I don't know," Harold repeated. "This is all very depressing."

"How about a big raise? Tell you what, I'll give you a twenty percent raise."

"I still think I would be depressed," said Harold.

"Fifty percent!" said DeCarlo. "I'll give you a fifty percent raise. Just please don't kill yourself."

"I don't know. I kind of had my heart set on it."

"Double!" shouted DeCarlo. "I'm going to double your salary. Surely you can't be depressed after double?"

"I guess a double might make me less depressed," said Harold, still thinking it over.

"A double it is." said DeCarlo. "Please don't kill yourself, Harold."

"Well, okay..."

DeCarlo stepped into Mr. Lee's office. Mr. Lee put down the spreadsheet he had been reviewing.

"How did it go with Harold?" asked Mr. Lee.

"I actually decided not to fire Harold... Harold stays," DeCarlo said, nodding authoritatively.

"Okay," said Mr. Lee. "You're still going to have to fire someone today."

DeCarlo squirmed. "And actually... We'll be giving Harold a raise. A pretty big one."

"How big?"

"Double."

"Dammit, DeCarlo, now you have to fire *two* people!"

DeCarlo nodded. "What two people do you think are *not* suicidal?"

DeCarlo ended up firing Stacey with the sass, and Stephen with the pranks. Stacey used the F-word in ways he had never heard before. She used it as a noun, verb, adjective, adverb, and occasionally as punctuation. She said some horrible things about DeCarlo's wife.

Stephen with the pranks simply stormed out of the office without saying a word. Shortly after, DeCarlo's wife called to say that a FedEx package had arrived at their home. DeCarlo told her not to open it.

Things were back to normal.

My Sweetest Angel

Marsha Webb

My Sweetest Angel,

I guess if you are reading this the worst has happened. I am so sorry I cannot be with you in person to answer your questions, to kiss away your tears or just to tell you that I love you.

I need to explain things to you and tell you the truth about what happened. I want to be totally honest with you. I got myself into trouble, a lot of trouble and I had nobody to help me. I am not making excuses for myself I just wanted to tell you exactly how it was.

I became friends with some people I should have stayed away from. I thought they were exciting and glamourous but it turned out they were dangerous, very dangerous. They sold drugs and made a lot of money; they commanded respect wherever they went. They carried guns and were not afraid to use them. I started dating the leader of the group, Charlie. Nobody messed with him, he fought like an animal, never lost a fight but he never laid a finger on me. He said I calmed him down, had a peaceful effect on him.

Although fun and exciting in the beginning, it wasn't any sort of long term life. People back and forth all the time, partying all night, alcohol and drugs everyday soon took its toll on me. Keeping a gun in my handbag was as normal as keeping my purse there. My family gave me warning after warning; they begged me to come home with them. Eventually they got so distressed at seeing me drunk or high they cut me off. Friends eventually fell away too.

After a number of years of living like that I knew I had had enough. I spoke to Charlie about us moving away from the big city, away from all the temptations. About us finding a small cottage in the country and settling down to some sort of normal life, but I guess Charlie loved his life, the danger, the respect he commanded and the status he had more than he loved me.

I resented this and felt I deserved more, felt I deserved something from being with him that long, all the things I did for him, those drop offs, the "meetings" I would have with the most terrifying people imaginable but I never once said no to Charlie, I loved him. So I planned an idea for a few weeks and decided to take what I thought I had earned; my gun, five grand in cash and his most expensive watch.

Charlie loved watches like women loved shoes, he had close on one hundred watches. He would spend longer deciding on what watch to wear than picking out his actual outfit. I had been around him long enough to know which was the most expensive watch, the Patek Philippe. It was worth around thirty thousand. Yes thirty thousand for a watch!

My plan was to get away somewhere quiet, a little village in the country and rent using the cash until I could find somewhere that would buy the watch then I could put a down payment on a home. I was hoping to get a job, maybe working in a shop or a tea room and start my life again, a nice normal life.

It didn't work though, I got caught. I was let down, you don't need to know all the details about that. I have never seen Charlie so cold, he stood and watched his gun trained on me as two of his henchmen punched and kicked me black and blue. I never took my eyes off him, I expected him to pull them off me and cradle me in his arms but he just stood and watched. I begged and I screamed for them to stop, I sobbed my heart out for Charlie to help, but nobody listened. The worst part of it all was that Charlie knew about you.

To cut a long story short I woke up in hospital. The nurses said I had been found unconscious in the street by a passer-by. I don't know if they dragged me out into the street like a piece of rubbish or if I had managed to crawl out to try and get help.

I was in hospital ten days in total with various broken bones, concussion and other injuries. I had no messages or visitors the whole time, except on the last day when the nurses had arranged for someone to come in to talk about you.

I tried to be brave but I cried a lot that day. I cried for the person I used to be, the person I could have been, the family and friends I had lost, the mistakes I had made, but most of all I cried for you.

To be fair the nurses were brilliant, they contacted the council for me and found me a place to stay. It was nothing like my cottage I had dreamed of; in fact it was the opposite. It was a noisy eighth floor flat in a tower block. The living room and kitchen were all in one tiny space and there was just enough room for a bed in the adjoining room. The carpets and walls were covered in stains and it smelled of damp. Still, I couldn't complain. I was safe and warm. I kept myself to myself, although an elderly woman, Eileen, living two doors down made it her duty to check up on me. She would often pop in telling me she had made too much casserole or pot roast and that if I didn't take it, it would end up in the bin. I was so grateful for the hot meals but more grateful for her kindness. It was Eileen who rang 999 and came with me to the hospital a few months later when she found me leaning against the lift doors barely able to stand unaided.

I told her over and over in the ambulance how scared I was. She reassured me and told me I was going to be fine and that she would not let anything bad happen to me, she held my hand all the way.

I know you don't remember but saying goodbye to you was the hardest thing I have ever had to do. I loved you then and I knew that I would always love you. As I held you I wondered what you would make of yourself and I prayed, yes I prayed to God that you would be safe and that you would have a much better life than I did.

I fought back the tears; I tried so hard to be brave as I touched your tiny fingers for the last time. "Be happy beautiful." I whispered to you as I handed you over, the nurse squeezed my shoulder and said "You are doing the right thing, that beautiful baby will be with loving family who want her so desperately and will give her everything". Despite my heart breaking in two within me, I knew she was right.

So I hope you are happy and have all the good things you deserve, but mostly I hope you will forgive me for letting you go. I only agreed because with all my heart I knew you would have a better life without me.

Your ever loving mother,

Rachel.

Stripes

Marsha Webb

Jamie held the grubby, grey cloth and slowly opened it to reveal his greatest treasure, his grandfather's medals. The medals calmed Jamie, helped him remember a time when he was safe and happy.

His mother was an alcoholic, he had never met his dad, who hadn't stayed around when his mum broke the news of her pregnancy. Jamie had often wondered why his mother had bothered to keep him, he always felt in the way. His beloved grandfather passed when Jamie was twelve years old and he was in a care home within six months. There he stayed until he was sixteen.

Jamie checked the time, 8.00pm; he was meeting Mick and the gang at 9.00pm. He slowly ran his fingers one more time over the medals, sighed involuntary and wrapped his prize possessions back up tightly. Pulling on his hoody and boots Jamie `s mind wandered to the past. He was seven years old, sat on his grandfather's knee, a biscuit in each hand.

"Tell me about your stripes grandad". His grandfather told him about all the countries he visited with the navy, what life was like, the food he had eaten, the people he had met. Jamie was fascinated; but his eyes would always be fixed on the gleam of the medals.

Jamie locked his tiny bedsit door, his stomach churned; he was feeling trepidation. It was his initiation, if he proved himself he would be accepted, part of the group, part of the family. Jamie didn't have anyone who looked out for him; in fact his grandfather had been the only person in his life that had ever looked out for him. He still felt the physical pain of loss all these years later.

While Jamie had been looking around the area social services had decided he should live, he wandered into The Half Moon pub. A rich looking couple at the bar complaining about everything, looked at Jamie like he was something they stepped in.

"We are never coming back to such a filthy hovel with such low life clientele". The man looked in Jamie's direction as he spat out the last statement.

Jamie looked away humiliated then caught sight of Mick, taking it all in, eyebrows raised, head thoughtfully to one side. The couple went to make their pointed exit; Mick stood up and bumped into the man.

"Oh, I'm so sorry". He bent down and picked up the man's wallet and handed it back. The couple left muttering. Mick handed Jamie a twenty pound note "Compensation mate" he grinned. Jamie was shocked and slightly impressed how quickly he had taken the money from the wallet. "Mick," he said by way of an introduction and stuck out his hand.

After a few drinks with Mick, Jamie took his number and arranged to meet up with him in town the next day. Although Jamie had been apprehensive Mick had won him over, he was charismatic and a born leader, he introduced Jamie to the rest of the gang. They seemed suspicious of him but Mick ensured he was welcomed and included. Jamie watched in awe as they targeted their victims taking wallets, phones, watches, purses and jewellery with the deftness of a hunting falcon.

Mick explained they picked out the rich, looking for designer clothing, apparently shoes and bags were the first things to look at. Jamie must have looked hesitant because Mick justified their actions saying that rich people had plenty of insurance and could replace their goods easily and it was their own fault for rubbing their riches in the faces of the poor. They started to meet up regularly. For the first time in a long time Jamie felt like he belonged somewhere.

Jamie shook his mind back to the present; he was almost outside the theatre where they had arranged to meet. Mick had told him all the rich people went to the theatre, it would be easy pickings. Despite his social services upbringing stealing didn't come easy to him, for some reason he had a strong moral compass despite everything he had been through.

The gang were waiting for him and in high spirits, they had already been drinking.

"There he is, ready for initiation day? Ready to prove yourself my boy?" Mick reached out to greet him. They horsed around for a while but Jamie's heart wasn't in it, he just wanted it over with, in truth he didn't want to do it at all.

Mick nudged him, "She`s the one." He pointed towards a well-dressed woman in her late sixties. "No" Jamie furrowed his brow "She`s too old".

"She`s loaded, look at her, you're only taking her purse, she won't miss a few quid".

Jamie was about to refuse again when Mick pushed him into her "Now."

Jamie stumbled, taken by surprise his elbow collided with her face, he overbalanced and forced her to the floor. She fell back heavily and her head thudded against the ground. Her shocked look was now forever etched into his mind. Her eyes rolled back, there was swelling around her eye already where his elbow had connected with her.

"Grab it and run" Mick shouted. Jamie hovered over her; he could see people running towards them. Instinct kicked in, he reached into her bag, grabbed the purse and ran after Mick who was already some distance away.

"Open it, how much you got?" Mick panted as they came to a stop a sufficient distance from town. Jamie's hands shook as he handed Mick the purse.

"Two hundred quid, well done mate". Jamie's eyes were fixed on the family photographs in her purse. Mick threw it and tucked the notes into his pocket.

"You've earned your stripes now". The words hit Jamie like a ton of falling bricks, his grandfather coming straight to his mind showing his stripes, his hard-earned sacrifices got him those medals. What would his grandfather think of him now?

Jamie hung his head in shame.

A Sunday Afternoon in Bandung

Justin Sanebridge

It was about 4 p.m. and everything was quiet, as is fitting on a Sunday afternoon in a quiet street.

My maid, Rina, squatted next to the kitchen entrance. She was eating. With her right hand she pushed rice and chicken into her mouth.

Rina thought she was about twenty years old. Her parents had already forgotten her year of birth. This often happens in the kampung, villages where two, sometimes three calendars are in use at the same time. There's the ancient Javanese calendar and the Gregorian, and then the Muslim calendar.

I was listening to baroque music in the living room.

Farther away, Indonesian pop songs sounded from a radio and then suddenly like a black oil slick the voice of the muezzin drifted over all the tunes. Half a minute later the muezzin of the other mosque started his call to prayer. A perfect cacophony arose. The baroque music and the pop songs were no longer heard.

The guys from the mosques shouted that Allah is great and Mohammed is his prophet. Especially in the early morning at 4am this call to prayer from several mosques drives me crazy. Can't they enjoy their religion in silence?

One of my friends is worse off than I. He lives in Jakarta next to a mosque and opposite a Protestant church.

When the mosque is silent, the fifty-member church choir starts singing psalms accompanied by a loud electric organ. On Sundays, the church bells ring. When the religious noise starts, my friend cannot even make phone calls anymore, because he can't hear the voice of his correspondent.

Suddenly I heard a man's harsh voice roaring at Rina. When I went into the kitchen to investigate, a shabbily dressed man stopped yelling at Rina and turned his attention and a vicious looking big sickle to me.

I am not a hero, but I remained calm.

In a slightly shaky voice, I asked him why he was so angry.

He gestured at Rina with his sickle.

"Mister has made my wife pregnant," he shouted.

His words struck me as the pointe of a good joke. The situation was so funny that I was no longer afraid. I could no longer restrain myself. I started to laugh. It was funny that he spoke to me so politely, but an Indonesian cannot resist that, the politeness towards an older person and an employer is ingrained in their language and culture, but I thought it was even much funnier that he thought that I had impregnated his wife.

He could not, of course, know that I had undergone a vasectomy the previous year. It would have surprised me if he knew what a vasectomy is.

Stunned, the man looked at me. I saw utter confusion in his eyes. He simply couldn't fathom why I was laughing.

"Come on," I said. "What do you want to drink? Tea? Coffee? Arak? Beer?"

He no longer smelled fear and intuitively sensed that I now had the upper hand.

I pulled him into my living room and offered him a chair.

Rina fell back in her role of pembantu (domestic servant) and served tea for him and a beer for me.

Nobody spoke a word.

I looked at Rina for a moment. She had indeed become more plump lately. Would she really be pregnant? But who would be the culprit?

Then I started my speech.

I addressed him as *Mas*, which means "brother", a very polite way of addressing a man in Indonesian.

The man shuffled a bit uncomfortably on the chair. He clearly preferred to sit on the floor.

I told him that I have so many willing girlfriends that I didn't even look at his wife. In order not to offend him, I casually mentioned that although his wife was not ugly, I was not interested in her. I also threw an Islamic sauce over it by quoting a few verses from the Holy Quran - in Arabic. Something like this is always successful with Muslims.

The man relaxed and drank his tea.

He just nodded and never said a word.

It was not so easy for him to express himself in Indonesian because his native language was Low Sundanese. He didn't understand High Sundanese.

"We are going to conclude an agreement." I said in Indonesian, "If the child looks like a mixed-race baby you may kill me, OK? Come back in about seven months."

He nodded.

He finally opened his mouth to apologize for his savage behavior and left.

He had just left the house when I was already in the kitchen.

"Rina," I asked, "Who has made you pregnant?"

Rina laughed shyly and said nothing.

I now knew she wouldn't tell me anything. There was no point in insisting.

She smiled the kind of meaningless smiles that are so typical of Indonesians and that sometimes drives me mad.

I looked at her with different eyes for a moment.

As she stood there in front of me with her eyes on the floor in a *sarong* that enveloped her chubby belly, she wasn't really ugly at all.

But who had given her that chubby belly?

About seven months later, Rina was ready to give birth. Around that time I had to fly to Jakarta to meet a businessman from Belgium.

I gave Rina a lot of money so that she could give birth in a hospital. She eagerly accepted the money and wished me a good trip.

Three days later I returned home.

Rina had put the money in her pocket, of course she hadn't wasted money on doctors and she had given birth in my kitchen with the help of an old woman from the neighborhood. According to the neighbour her son looked 100 percent Indonesian. A big and healthy Indonesian baby.

I never saw her husband or Rina again. Two days after the birth she had suddenly disappeared. And my gardener had disappeared too…

A day in August

Justin Sanebridge

That day in August, thousands of Belgians complained about the heat. 'I wish it were already autumn', many people would say.

A big, fat man of about forty had said that same sentence in a pub in the city centre of Antwerp.

Next to him, three other men stood at the bar. They were in their forties and judging by their expensive suits, rather wealthy.

"Look over there, Jan," said a tall skinny man. "That bloke doesn't seem to suffer from the hot weather."

He pointed at an old gentleman who had just arrived. The man was dressed in a brown three-piece suit that had gone out of fashion before 1950 and he had an Al Capone hat on his head.

"Well, Grandpa." Jan said. "Isn't it warm enough for you?"

The little man showed a shy smile and said in an amazingly clear voice "I'm fine, I'm fine."

Then he sat down at a table by the window, took off his hat, and carefully placed it on the empty chair beside him.

"A Trappist beer, please, sir." he said politely to the bartender.

"Look here," Jan laughed, "grandfather drinks strong beer!"

They all laughed as if they saw a child doing something adulty. The old man nodded benevolently and then looked out the window.

The conversation continued at the bar. The boys were no longer interested in the old man.

"Tell me, Jan," a bearded guy asked, "Were you not bothered by the heat in Indonesia?"

Glad that he was offered an opportunity to boast about his vacation, Jan said in a teaching tone: "No, it's a different kind of heat there. It's not like here in summer."

"Hot women over there?" asked another friend making an obscene gesture.

They all laughed.

"Come on, Jan, tell me." said the bearded guy, "And give me some addresses because next year I might go to Indonesia"

"Oh man," said Jan. "That's impossible to explain. You must have been there to understand that. They only live to fuck, eat and sleep. In that order. And they can take care of a guy, the women over here can learn something from them!"

The old gentleman took a deep breath and sighed inaudibly. Carefully, in jerks, he let the air escape through his nostrils. Then he took a sip of the strong Trappist beer and closed his eyes for a moment.

She was so beautiful, my Sarinah from that small village. Her long jet black hair, her nice nose, her perfect young breasts. I was also so young, so very young. I was eighteen. Take her as a housekeeper, the Dutch said, you don't marry a native girl, do you? Enjoy her and kick her out when you become tired of her.

No, I didn't listen to them. I married her, and it was a great party too, without any white people. Oh correction, there were white people. My parents were there. My Dad and my Mum were more understanding than their contemporaries. They had nothing against me marrying a native girl. Well, my father also had Indonesian sweethearts, and my mother knew that, but she didn't complain. That's how one lived in those days in colonial Indonesia.

Sarinah, you've been dead a long time and I can't even go to your grave because you don't have one. You were shot to pieces by a Japanese machine gun when you slapped the cheek of a Japanese soldier. That Jap who hit me when I had to march to the camp with all those other Dutch people. You couldn't stand that, and you hit that Jap in the face. Immediately our child in your belly who was blissfully waiting to be born was also killed.

The old gentleman was suddenly taken back to the present by Jan's loud and drunken voice.

Convinced of his expertise, Jan continued: "I also went to a so-called Health Resort. The end! The service! Unbelievable! You get a massage, a bath, another massage, anyway, fantastic. I paid a little extra and I got to fuck two girls over there, ha! Incredible!"

The old man took another sip from his strong Belgian beer.

A health resort. We were so happy when the Japanese soldiers told us in the camp of Changi that we were going to a health resort! They said we could bring records. The Japanese would provide gramophones.

136

How many died in the cattle cars of that train? Five days on that train and so may corpses every day. And how many died during that long march on foot through the jungle? Three hundred kilometers on foot from Bampong in Thailand to Number Two camp in Songkurai, and that's where hell really started. The sick received half portions because they could not work. "No work, no food." said the Japanese.

In that health resort we worked from 5 a.m. to 9 p.m., and sometimes even later. Then came the cholera. Fifty comrades died every day. The Japs laughed: how many are dead today?

And we had to keep working, always working harder.

Then came beriberi, dysentery, diphtheria, smallpox, tropical wounds.

We were dragged out of our beds by our hair, beaten with bamboo sticks, laughed at.

A health resort ... they had promised.

That camp near Bandung in Indonesia, where we had to wait for transport to Singapore. Arifin, my friend Ari. And also Udin, my good friend. All the food you brought to the camp in Cimahi and put it under the barbed wire. My beautiful Indonesian friends. Heroes. And then your heads, cut off with a sword. Your heads rolling in the dust in a fountain of blood. We were forced to look at the execution. Ten of us were also selected. Ten white heads off. The Japs wanted to set an example. See, that happens if you don't follow our rules. Natives and whites, all equal: head off.

Watch out, no, well, too late, I still can't hold back those tears. I'll order another beer.

The guys were just starting out on the topic of "hot women in Thailand" when an old tall lady came in. You could see that she must have been a beauty once. Even as an old lady she was beautiful, well-groomed, distinguished, with fine Eurasian characteristics, half Indonesian and some Portuguese blood. She was slender and graceful.

She went to the table of the little man.

Everyone at the bar, including the bartender, looked at her. They couldn't do more than watch, because they didn't understand a word of the conversation.

"Darling, are you crying now?" She spoke Indonesian. "Everything went well at the hospital, I don't have cancer. The doctors said that I will be with you for a long time. Come on, drink up, we'll eat mussels somewhere. "

The old man stood up and hugged his wife.

"Ah Widya", he said in Indonesian. "Sometimes I'm such an old, dreary guy. Where would I be without you?"

He stood up and hugged his wife.

He threw some money on the table and they walked hand in hand into the warm street.

Afterword

Roo B. Doo

2019 was generally considered a whacked out, fucked up and completely bonkers year, Dear Reader. Then 2020 arrived with a polite request to 'Hold my bottle of Corona...'

Today is Easter Monday, and as I write, the majority of the global population are locked in their homes, patiently waiting for curves to flatten and Coronavirus cures to be found, so that they get out and get on with their normal lives. Currently there is no end in sight.

Hopefully we'll still be around for Underdog Anthology XII, due out in October, but in the meantime, Leg Iron Books have generously slashed the price of its Kindle offerings to 99p/99c, so there is no need to be bored. COVID-19 is a *novel* virus, doncha know ;)

https://legironbooks.co.uk/

Now for some more butchering...

Beloved children's author A.A. Milne authored the Winnie-the-Pooh books. The Public school, which his father ran and where little Alan Alexander grew up, employed H.G. Wells as a teacher. Herbert George famously wrote the novel 'War Of The Worlds' in which a thriving population was wiped out by a microorganism. If you're not at all familiar with that story, then apologies for the spoiler.

Fortunately, A.A. Milne was also a poet and now joins the ranks of Shakespeare, Blake, Lazarus et al. on the slab of an Underdog Anthology Dead Poets page, with a mutilation of his children's verse 'Now We Are Six'. It lends itself rather well to the current times...

Now We Are Sick

When it was One,
It had just begun.
When it was Two,
It was Wuhan Flu.
When it was Three
People start to flee.

When it was Four,
Italy at death's door.
When it was Five,
Boris is alive!
But now we are sick,
Locked down and Covid-clever,
So I think we'll be sick now for ever and ever.

Keep well, Dear Reader, and if you can't free your body, then free your mind.

About the Authors

Gayle Fidler

Gayle Fidler is a writer, collector of bad taxidermy, paranormal researcher, part time pirate and make-up artist. She is also a Viking blacksmith who likes to hand forge spoons and toasting forks.

Gayle lives in the North East of England with several cats and several children. She is married to her best friend Ben, who lives 100 miles away from her in Yorkshire because he likes to sleep with all the windows open.

Gayle began writing on the back of beer mats to try and make up reasonable excuses for some of the ridiculous situations her and Ben found themselves in during drunken capers.

Wandra Nomad

Born well infused – perhaps some would say overly infused – with wanderlust and curiosity, Wandra Nomad has traversed much of the globe, exploring a myriad of customs and cultures while participating in diverse opportunistic pursuits including a multitude of occupations that helped fund said treks.

Also born an unbridled dreamer, this wanderer has traveled even further in imagination. The results of this combination are innumerable diverse 'tales to be told', one of which is offered in this Anthology. There are more to come in Wandra's own collection, 'Musings of a Wanderer', very soon.

Having sampled a variety of climates ranging from freezing ice and snow to steaming jungles along the way a definite preference hasdeveloped. Today many such tales are spun by the Muse on the beaches around the tropical belt before wending their way to this nomad's keyboard.

Marsha Webb

Marsha lives just outside Cardiff and is a full time high school teacher. She has only recently started writing.

"Writing short stories are my favourite because teaching takes up so much time and because I love the feeling of achievement when a story is finished. I have always had a very over active imagination and writing allows me to use this in a positive way."

Marsha also has stories in Underdog Anthologies 6, 7, 8, 9 and 10 and has had a number of short stories and poems published in online magazines and themed anthologies.

Her first novel 'You Can Choose Your Sin… but you cannot choose the consequences' is now available in print and eBook formats.

Daniel Royer

Daniel Royer is a writer of short fiction. He is a California State University, Bakersfield graduate with an English Degree he's not using. Royer works as a full-time welder to support his true passion, which is tomahawk-throwing. His stories have been printed by Ponahakeola Press, SFReader.com, and some other publications you've never heard of. Royer lives in California. He has a cat.

Mark Ellott

Mark Ellott is a part time motorcycle instructor, delivering training for students who require compulsory basic training and direct access courses. He has retired from his main job as a freelance trainer and assessor working primarily in the rail industry, delivering track safety training and assessment as well as providing consultancy services in competence management.

He writes fiction in his spare time. Mostly, his fiction consists of short stories crossing a range of genres, and has stories in all but one of the previous Underdog Anthologies – and now in this one.

His first three novels, 'Ransom', 'Rebellion' and 'Resolution', are now available in print and eBook formats.

He has also published a volume of his own short stories, entitled 'Blackjack', and a collection of Morning Cloud Western stories entitled 'Sinistré'.

Roo B. Doo

'The Trouble With Tibbles' is a Coronavirus lock down story, Dear Reader, dedicated to a certain Mrs Splashett, who said nice things about my Harry Egg stories on Amazon. No doubt she's locked down too and could do with some cheering up.

Want more Roob? You can find her on the internet, ably assisted by Clicky, who may or may not be a) an alien dolphin and b) from another dimension, lolling about her Library of Libraries, writing synchromystic shambles at www.roobeedoo2.wordpress.com

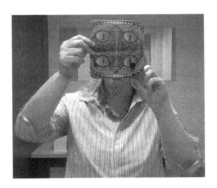

S. W. Duffy

I am a professor of cancer screening, living in Cambridge and working in London. I write poetry and short fiction in my spare time. Born in Scotland, I have lived in England for the past forty years. Although I have worked in several countries, the fiction seems usually to hark back to London. When I first went to London to do my MSc, I found the place mysterious and bewildering. Most of my stories seem to focus on the atmosphere of mystery which for me at least, pervades this overwhelming city. I shall always be grateful to Leg Iron Books for providing me with an outlet for the stories.

Justin Sanebridge

Justin Sanebridge is the author of "The Goddess of Protruding Ears." Now also available in Dutch as "De Godin van de Flaporen."

Some of his short stories have appeared in 'The Good, the Bad and Santa' (Underdog Anthology 4), 'Transgenre Dreams' (UA8) and in 'The Silence of the Elves' (UA10).

Somewhat reclusive, he prefers not to be photographed so has elected to be represented by a stone with eyes.

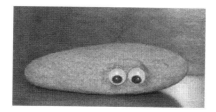

H. K. Hillman

H. K. Hillman is the creator, or perhaps creation, of Romulus Crowe, Dr. Phineas Dume and Legiron the Underdog. Now pretty much retired from science, he hides out in an ancient farmhouse in Scotland with a Viking who calls herself CynaraeStMary. The house includes a skull in a holly tree, a gallows stone in the wall and holy water comes out of all the taps.

Here he spends a lot of time thinking up horrible stories, and running the tiny publishing house called Leg Iron Books, helped by Roo B. Doo, who he's never met.

No, he doesn't understand how any of this happened either.

LEG IRON BOOKS

Also available from Leg Iron Books:

Underdog Anthologies

'The Underdog Anthology, volume 1'
'Tales the Hollow Bunnies Tell' (anthology II)
'Treeskull Stories' (anthology III)
'The Good, the Bad and Santa' (anthology IV)
'Six in Five in Four' (anthology V)
'The Gallows stone' (anthology VI)
'Christmas Lights… and Darks' (anthology VII)
'Transgenre Dreams' (anthology VIII)
'Well Haunted' (anthology IX)
'The Silence of the Elves' (anthology X)
   All edited by H.K. Hillman and Roo B. Doo.

Fiction

'The Goddess of Protruding Ears' by Justin Sanebridge.
'De Godin van de Flaporen' by Justin Sanebridge (in Dutch)
'Ransom', by Mark Ellott
'Rebellion' by Mark Ellott
'Resolution' by Mark Ellott
'Blackjack' a collection of short stories by Mark Ellott.
'Sinistré (The Morning Cloud Chronicles)' by Mark Ellott
'The Mark' by Margo Jackson
'You'll be Fine' by Lee Bidgood
'Feesten onder de Drinkboom' by Dirk Vleugels (in Dutch)
'Es-Tu là, Allah?' by Dirk Vleugels (in French)
'Jessica's Trap' by H.K. Hillman
'Samuel's Girl' by H.K. Hillman
'Norman's House' by H. K. Hillman
'The Articles of Dume' by H.K. Hillman
'Fears of the Old and the New' short stories by H.K. Hillman

'Dark Thoughts and Demons' short stories by H.K. Hillman
'You Can Choose Your Sin… but You Cannot Choose the Consequences' by Marsha Webb.

Non-fiction:

'Ghosthunting for the Sensible Investigator' first and second editions, by Romulus Crowe.

Biography:

'Han Snel' by Dirk Vleugels (in Dutch).

Printed in Great Britain
by Amazon